Mornin' Star Risin'

Jean E. Holmes

Pacific Press Publishing Association
Boise, Idaho
Oshawa, Ontario, Canada

Edited by Marvin Moore
Designed by Dennis Ferree
Cover by Mark Stutzman
Typeset in 10/12 Century Schoolbook

Copyright © 1992 by
Pacific Press Publishing Association
Printed in United States of America
All Rights Reserved

Library of Congress Cataloging-in-Publication Data:
Holmes, Jean E., 1942-
    Mornin' star risin': master and slave struggle against
spiritual ignorance and social injustice / Jean Holms: [ed-
ited by Marvin Moore].
      p.   cm.
    Includes bibliographical references (pp. 159, 160).
    ISBN 0-8163-1064-5
    1. South Carolina—History—1775-1865—Fiction. 2. Sea
Islands—History—Fiction. I. Moore, Marvin, 1937- . II.
Title. III. Title: Morning star rising.
PS3558.035937M6   1992
813'.54—dc20
                                        919-29460
                                            CIP

04 05 06 07 08 • 8 7 6 5 4

Contents

Introduction

Mornin' Star Risin' is a historic narrative set in the tranquil beauty of the South Carolina Sea Islands during the decade immediately prior to the Civil War. It is the story of two diverse groups of people—masters and slaves—struggling against the evils of spiritual ignorance, social injustice, and physical bondage.

The story began, however, in a land far removed from the wide marshes and fertile barrier islands of South Carolina's "Low Country." From the Windward Coast of Africa, from countries such as Senegal, Sierra Leone, and present-day Liberia, the Gullah people came. In their homelands they had been known as rice planters, experts in the cultivation of a crop difficult to grow, but in great demand worldwide. Their coming to the southeastern shores of America was by no choice of their own. Like so many of their fellow Africans, they crossed the Atlantic chained together and stacked like cordwood in the stinking holds of nefarious ships known as "slavers." This, however, was only the beginning of the dehumanization process enforced upon them by the institution of slavery.

The value of the African rice growers significantly increased once they reached the slave markets of Charleston and Savannah. Unlike their counterparts from other areas of Africa, they were kept together. Communication within the slave community itself, though feared and at all costs avoided on southern plantations, was an essential element for the cultivation of rice. Thus the African rice growers maintained much of their original language. In time, though, the cultivation of rice gave way to the more productive, long-staple cotton, and the native language turned into an English-based Creole that was better suited to the demands of the new society in which the Gullahs lived. Yet the original flavor of both the language and the culture was retained.

Today the value of the colorful expressions and musical language of the Gullah peoples is finally being recognized. For many years following the Civil War, the Gullahs were told to hide their dialectic difference. Leaders and educators alike shamed them into believing that it was simply "bad English." A recent increase in sociological research, however, has uncovered the fascinating link of heritage between the Krio language of Sierra Leone and the Gullah dialect of the Sea Islands. Wycliffe Bible translators have launched an ambitious program to produce a Gullah version of the Scriptures. Gullah festivals and a rash of media presentations have brought this transplanted people and their language to the forefront.

Because the Gullahs were isolated on the Sea Islands, often outnumbering their white masters in population by more than a hundred to one, many of their African cultural practices were also retained. The link between ancient African religions and the practice of Christianity was apparent. The pagan aspects of these ancient religions—voodoo, witchcraft, and devil worship—were very much a part of life within the slave communities of the 1700s and 1800s.

I have made no attempt to soften this fact for the refined tastes of the modern-day Christian reader. Witchcraft and sorcery brought with them fear, and the "Christians" of the plantation societies certainly made no effort to soften that fact. They used that fear as a tool to control their slaves.

Neither have I sought to completely strip the Gullah dialect from the text, though I have modified it considerably for readability. My purpose was not to demean the speakers, but to retain the flavor of their language. Nor have I eliminated words and titles such as *nigger, buck, buckra, boy,* etc. These were unquestionably racial slurs, meant at the time to demean. As such, they were and still are repulsive and reprehensible. I myself find them highly repulsive. But this is the story of slavery, and its disgraceful nature must not be glossed over. My purpose is to show how a group of determined people were able to rise above both their pagan religion and demeaning slavery to become a proud and unique cultural community, strong in Christian faith and patriotic zeal.

Finally, this is the story of the slave masters. It is not, however, a rehash of *Uncle Tom's Cabin.* The white planters were not all "devils" out to degrade the African men and women purchased as laborers for their land holdings. On the whole it was the *institution* of slavery, and not the individual slave owner, that was evil. There were, of course, a few—as there were within the slave community itself—who used this power wrongly. Many, however, looked upon their "people" as friends and protectors. They respected them as fellow humans; they encouraged their children to learn from them; they laughed in their hours of celebration and wept at their times of loss. More important, as time passed and attitudes changed, at least a few of those who had been masters returned to the beautiful lands of the Sea Islands to become willing servers to those who had once been slaves. This is their story too.

Some readers may wonder whether *Mornin' Star Risin'* is a true story. Not in the sense that every detail happened the way I wrote it. Seldom is that true, even of a biography. I have spent many years doing historical research on the Gullah people, and I have collected many boxes of material. The book is based on this research. While the specific plantation that I describe did not exist during the decade prior to the Civil War, many of the events in the story did happen, and many of the characters are real. In some cases events were so real and so emotionally charged at the time they occurred that even now, nearly 150 years later, I have disguised some of the details in order to avoid creating problems for living descendants.

In one sense the story that you will read in *Mornin' Star Risin'* is unique because it happened to the Gullah people and their slave masters. But in a wider sense it is universal. Its joys and its sorrows, its victories and its defeats, have been experienced in every age since time began. Beyond the struggle that you read in this book and that each of us experiences in our everyday life, we can see the blessed hope that one day all who truly love the Lord will stand as equals and sing together the jubilant songs of freedom.

Acknowledgments

I count it a privilege to personally thank the many dedicated people who have shared their time and knowledge to make this book possible. Tita Heins, a Gullah speaker and storyteller affectionately known as "Aunt Tita" throughout much of the South as well as in her Low Country homeland, has done far more than assist me with dialect and cultural practices. She has also been a willing hostess and a close friend. Pat Sharpe, a linguist with the Wycliffe Bible Translators on St. Helena's Island, South Carolina, assisted me in finding the people and resources needed for the research on this book. Gerhart Spieler, a newspaper columnist and historian in Beaufort County, South Carolina, has provided both historical proofreading services and large amounts of resource material. Phyllis Dolislager, who gave of herself unstintingly to critique and proofread every page of this work, has proved herself a friend *par excellence*. Her deep faith and Christlike perspectives have often been the driving force behind my humble efforts. Finally, I wish to thank my husband, Lucien Holmes, native son of South Carolina. It was he who first introduced me to the Sea Islands and afforded me the time and freedom to travel over their length and breadth so that I, too, might share his deep love for the people and the land.

Dedication

In memory of a loving mother,
who taught me the meaning of freedom.

1
Drum Beats

(1850)

Streaks of red and black war paint glistened on the faces of the braves as they leaped and danced around the flames. Long tongues of fire licked at their muscular legs. Their coiled topknots, encrusted with vermillion paint, swung to and fro as they danced. In and out of the flames they moved, their bodies twisting and turning through waves of shimmering heat.

The pulsating sound of drums grew ominous as the figure of a man in a robe of white egret feathers approached. His masked face, grotesque in the firelight, was that of a bird of prey. Only his eyes could be seen, their black depths reflecting the tongues of flame until they seemed to burn of their own accord. He waited as though poised for flight; then, with the shrill cry of a hunting eagle, he plunged through the line of dancing Indians.

Chanting in time with the drums, the birdlike figure raised his arms over the burning coals. Slowly his clenched fists uncurled, and the fire exploded in a spray of brilliant light and flying sparks. Waves of heat and leaping flames shot upward, lifting the braves as they writhed about in their macabre dance.

The masked figure turned, this time beckoning the boy, calling out his name, "Gil-ly, come. Come, Gil-ly. Come!"

"Come on, Gilly! Wake up, son. You're dreaming. There's nothing to be afraid of."

Eight-year-old Gilly opened his eyes. His mother stood over him, her smile gentle with concern. She reached down and stroked back a lock of his damp hair. As she touched his face, the soft fabric of her white gown rubbed against his cheek. With a shudder, he pulled away, seeing again the feathered robe of his nightmare.

"It's all right, Gilly. It's over. I'm with you now."

"There were drums, Mama. Did you hear them? I'm sure there were drums."

"Oh, no, child, there were no drums. It's just the sound of the waves hitting the pier. You were sleeping—you had a bad dream. It's over now."

The woman turned at the sound of footsteps. Her husband stood behind her, his stern face angular in the candlelight. "The boy's right, Marian. Why fool him? There *are* drums; I've heard them every night for more than a week." He turned away and pounded his fist into his hand. "We'll have to put a stop to this. It's getting out of hand!"

Marian Weldon protectively encircled the child with her arms. "Please, Gilbert, he's far too young to understand. Why frighten him more?"

Gilly felt his mother's body tremble and knew that it was she who was afraid. Why? What did it mean? Where was the sound of the drums coming from?

The boy had reason to wonder at his father's agitation. Gilbert Weldon was a man who prided himself on his self-control, but this was different. It wasn't anger he felt. It was more than that—an explosive mixture of frustration and, though he'd never admit it, a niggling fear.

Tightly cinching the sash of his robe, Gilbert walked to the window and peered into the darkness. He cocked an ear and listened for the distant mutter of the drums. It was the slaves; he was certain of that. The sounds were coming from Ladies Island. He could only hope that none of his people was involved. The patrol was sure to catch them tonight. If not, they'd be forced to call in the militia. Nothing struck terror into the hearts of the planters on these lonely islands quite as much as the thought of a slave rebellion. If the blacks once realized that they could overwhelm their masters by sheer numbers, there would be a blood bath!

While the master of Weldon Oaks fretted over the problem of the drums, his young son fought back sleep with an imagination made more vivid by the candlelight and the echoing sounds coming from the darkened forest. A slave rebellion was the furthest thing from his mind. He had never given serious thought to the social status of the Negroes. They were just there—like the house and the fields. It was the Indians who filled his nightly dreams. Their shadowy forms danced across the walls, and their ghostly faces leered at him with every beam of moonlight that filtered through the shuttered windows.

It was Gullah Jim who had stirred Gilly's imagination with his spellbinding stories. And how he could tell them!—as though he had been there himself those many years ago when the Yemassees and Guales streaked their faces with war paint and sharpened the long, curved blades of their scalping knives. If a boy listened with more than his ears, he found himself there too. Gilly let his eyelids droop and close. In his mind he could hear Jim's musical voice telling of that fateful day when the Yemassees had come to Coosaw.

"Ki! Dat ben many a year gone by. Many a year!" The old man's lilting voice, laced with the words and nuances of his West African heritage, gently touched his listener's ear. "What year be dis?" he asked.

"Eighteen-fifty," answered Gilly, proud of possessing such knowledge.

"Dat's right den, many a year gone by. De buckra—" at this, the old black looked sideways to see if the boy comprehended. "De white man don't hab many slaves back den, but me-oh-my, dey sho got Injuns." Jim rolled his eyes for effect. "Lots and lots ob Injuns!

"Happen dis-a-way. Yemassees—dat ben de name of dese

Injuns—Yemassees get tired ob all de promises giben—neber kept. Tired of de buckra stealin' de land, cuttin' de trees, damin' de creeks. One day all dose Injuns get demselbes togeda an' commences fer ta fight . . ."

And so old Jim told and retold the story. Gilly could repeat it by heart. More than that, with his eyes closed and his mind drifting back—back in time—he could see it all happening.

The small farmstead lay nestled among the pines, the spring sunshine softening the sharp edges of its crude buildings with the pale light of early morning. The homesteader placed the last baskets of salted fish and smoked meat in his flat-bottomed bateau. He would barter them in Port Royal for the seed he needed for spring planting. Rubbing the remnants of salt from his hands onto the stiff fabric of his breeches, he reached out and touched his young bride's face and then brushed her cheek with a gentle kiss.

For a long moment, they stood there looking into each other's eyes. Then, sensing the start of her tears, he turned away abruptly, fearful that any further hesitation would undo his purpose. He stepped into his boat and, with a final wave, poled the awkward craft away from the bank until the pull of the current took it to midstream.

The young woman standing on the muddy bank shaded her eyes from the shimmering glare of sunlight on the moving water. She watched intently as the small boat reached the distant bend in the river. As it slowly drifted out of sight, she lifted her arm in farewell. Blinded by the brightness of the water, she was oblivious to the long dugout canoes skulking among the shadows on the opposite shore.

The Yemassees, their faces smeared with black and red paint, the symbols of war and death, bode their time until a restless flock of white egrets resettled themselves on the frilly branches of the tall cypress that marked the far bend in the river. When all was quiet, the braves moved out across the water, leaving hardly a ripple to mark their passage. A swarm of buzzing flies followed in their wake, attracted by the dried blood on the scalping knives and the gruesome remnants of human hair that dangled from the deerskin belts of the war party.

The small group of braves crept silently toward the newly built cabin under the pines. The woman was alone. One of the braves, the leader of the group, made a quick decision and motioned his men to put up their knives. Approaching the cowering woman, his mouth twisted in a menacing sneer, he reached out and grasped a lock of her shining auburn hair. Twisting the strands of hair around his hand as one would appraise a skein of new yarn, he grunted and pointed to the river. For the time being she would be more useful to them alive. The brave nearest the leader moved with the swiftness of a springing panther. He bound the woman's hands and dragged her to his waiting canoe.

Terrified of what was to become of her, the woman could do no more than lie in the bottom of the canoe and watch the destruction of the island homesite that she and her husband had worked so hard to build. It was with a resigned certainty that she knew she would never see it again.

The farm animals—the milk cow, the hogs, the old mule, and the squawking chickens—meant nothing to the Yemassees. They had the wealth of the forests and streams to choose from, but the lust for blood and revenge was upon them. Opening the pens, they slaughtered the helpless creatures within, wreaked havoc on the outbuildings, fired the main house, and carried off whatever implements they deemed valuable. Having finished their violent deed, they returned to their canoes and silently disappeared into the rising mists of the shadowy river.

Two days passed before the man returned. He sensed disaster even before rounding the bend. The sickening smell of smoke and carrion clung to the air. A flock of vultures rose at his approach, their thick bodies and long wings moving across the face of the sun to cast morbid, moving shadows on the water. His buildings were gone; smoldering piles of ashes marked the places where they had been.

As his foot touched the shore, the horrible smell of decaying flesh struck him, causing him to stumble backward. Feeling the bile rise in his throat, he pressed his hand across his face and willed himself to approach the animal pens. His mule and the milk cow lay where they had been slaughtered, their bodies bloated and flyblown. The hogs and chickens lay scattered about in the horrid confusion of panicked victims seeking to outrun the certainty of death.

There were moccasin prints everywhere—their toed-in patterns telling of those who had wreaked the carnage. Walking cautiously to the rubble that had once been his home, the man shuddered involuntarily, certain of what he would find in the ashes. Steeling himself, he took up a branch and raked through the charred wood but could find nothing resembling human remains.

Dropping the branch, he searched the shattered pens and storage bins. He skirted the creek bed and ran through the pine woods, shouting out her name, all the time hoping to find some small sign. But only the raucous calls of the scavenger birds answered him. Finally, with bowed head and heaving shoulders, he retraced his steps to the bank of the river. It was there, half-covered with mud, that he found her silk slipper.

". . . and it's time he learned." Gilly shook himself from the lifelike horror of his dream. His father was still talking. Pulling away from his mother's arms, he sat up on the edge of the bed. It was vital that he know about the drums. What if the savages came back to Coosaw?

"Papa, what do the drums mean? Will the Indians come back?"

Gilbert Weldon shook his head. His wife was right; he had no business scaring the boy with this talk of drums. "No, Gilly, the Indians have been gone for years."

"Where did they go, then?"

Gilbert lifted his son in his arms. "The tribe was scattered, son. Most of them joined the Creek nation in their migration to the mountains beyond the upcountry." He hesitated, thinking back to the stories that, in his own childhood, he so loved to hear. "I've heard it said that there were those who went south—down through the Okefenokee—or possibly all the way into Florida."

"Aren't there any left in the Low Country, then, Papa? Perhaps they've just gotten mixed up with some of our people."

Gilbert was startled by the boy's insight. How, at such a young age, had his son hit upon the one thought that so often added to his own fears of an uprising? It was common knowledge, of course, that slaves *did* escape from time to time. But the possibility that many of them might have joined with the Indian nations, eventually blending into a potentially fierce fighting force, was a matter not openly discussed. The red men had never taken well to the slave economy. With the two bloods mixed, and with revenge as their motive, they would be hard to stop.

Gilbert decided that in this case, evasion would be the best response. "It's possible, son, but not worth worrying about. In any case, I've heard that there are a few of them left in Yemassee Town, but they're a rather dispirited lot—poor as sharecroppers."

His wife reached out and took the boy in her arms once more. "Gilbert, you *must* talk to Jim. He's the one who's filling the child's head with tales. It's no wonder he has nightmares!"

"No, they're not just tales, Marian. Those stories are a part of his heritage. You mustn't be so hard on old Jim; he means well."

Gilly glanced at his father. So it was true; there were Indians. If so, surely it was they who talked at night with their drums. He tried to digest the information; but something didn't fit. Yemassee Town was miles away. Could the sound of drums carry so far?

Papa lifted Gilly up and stood him on the bed. He grasped his shoulders and made him stand straight and tall. "Son, you must never let fear overcome you. A strong man must first learn to master himself before he can be the master of others."

He waited for Gilly to nod his understanding and then continued. "There are things that, from time to time, you may question—things that don't seem entirely fair. But remember this: the inferior races were nothing more than savages before we civilized them."

Gilly looked at his father quizzically, wondering how such a nice conversation had suddenly turned into a lecture. What did his father mean by "inferior races"? Considering, however, the stern look that had come across Papa's face, perhaps it was better not to ask. But he was wide awake now and enjoying himself. Gilly decided to take a different tack. "What about the pirates, Papa? Gullah Jim said there used to be lots of pirates."

Gilbert Weldon let out a deep laugh. "I'm not a storyteller, son, not like old Jim. But I do know this: there's meaning to every story that he tells. They're not just idle tales! Oh, sometimes he'll make them sound that way—animals that talk and people who fly—but there's something real behind all of that imagination." He stopped and looked sideways at his wife, then quickly added, "Of course, animals don't talk like people, and people don't fly like birds. Jim knows that. Listen to him with your heart and not your head, son."

"Gilbert, please!" Marian Weldon's voice was laced with tears. The flickering candlelight accentuated the pallid lines of her face. "It's one o'clock in the morning. The boy needs his sleep!"

Gilbert stood up and gently placed his arm around his wife's sagging shoulders. "I'm sorry, Marian. Of course, you're right. We've had too many of these late nights." He bent down and pressed the boy back onto the soft goose-down mattress. "Gilly, you must try to go to sleep now. Your mama needs her rest, son. We'll be having a new baby in the house soon. Now, won't that be fine? You'll have a little brother or sister to play with."

Gilly sat upright and stuck out his lower lip. He didn't consider that "fine" at all. He was quite happy the way things were.

"This is quite enough for the night, Gilly," Mama said as she kissed him on the forehead. "Now close your eyes and go to sleep."

She blew out the candle by his bed, kissed him again, and then she and Gilbert tiptoed from the room. As they walked away, Gilly caught the first few sentences of their conversation.

"Marian, I'm going down to Maum Beezie's cabin in the morning. It's high time we had a children's nurse back here. She really should have stayed after helping with Gilly's birth. I know I can trust her. After all, she was my nurse when I was a child."

"I know you're right, but I hate to give up his care. Besides, Maum Beezie is growing older. Perhaps we should consider someone else. What about Josephine?"

"Indeed not! Josephine's talents obviously lie in the kitchen. I'll not have a perfectly good cook sent off to mind children."

"Then one of the young women from the quarters, perhaps one with small children."

"Marian, Maum Beezie may be growing older, but she knows how to handle children better than any field hand. Running a plantation house is no easy matter. This is not the time to be training field hands as nursemaids, especially when we have a perfectly good one in Maum Beezie. With another child on the way . . ."

Their voices trailed off down the hallway and disappeared. Gilly lay quietly for a while until the house grew still. He listened intently. There it was again, the thumping of the drums—and something else. Was it voices he heard in the wind, voices chanting in time with the drums?

He tiptoed through the shadowy room to the window and quietly slid it open. His bedroom faced east, and he could smell the salty breath of the sea in the freshening breeze. He stretched as far over the windowsill as he dared. There lay the river beyond the row of oaks, but the drum sounds were not coming from the direction of the river. They were coming from the south. If it were the Indians of Yemassee Town, surely he would hear them coming from up the river.

His gaze traveled from the river to the sky. High, thin clouds scudded along, covering the full moon, turning its light into a silver haze that glistened like frost on the massive live oaks. Long, thick shrouds of Spanish moss hung from the gnarled branches of the trees. The wind made them sway like tattered battle flags. Only the wind could be heard now. The thud of drums and the fainter sounds of chanting had stopped.

Suddenly the moon broke free from the clouds. A long, shimmering path of golden light stretched as far as his eye could see across the wide mouth of the Coosaw River. Gilly concentrated his gaze on the path of light, wondering if it would reveal a flotilla of war canoes or perhaps a pirate ship, but the river was empty. There was nothing; only the moonlight and the distant hunting cry of an osprey.

Gilly twisted around so that he could look to the south, the direction of the drums. Beyond the wide, dark lawns rose a forest of tall pines and oaks. Thickets of cedar and palmetto scrub clustered beneath the overhanging branches of the tall trees. The edges of the woods were dark and constantly moving with the winds that swept these small Sea Islands off the Carolina coast. When the wind came from the south or from the west, it smelled of the marshes and the forest, pungent and earthy. That was the smell that Papa liked best. But Gilly preferred the tangy smell of the ocean. It was clean and made him feel brave—brave like a pirate.

Pulling himself back in through the window, Gilly sat cross-legged on the cold floorboards. If it was not the Indians, then who was beating the drums? He stood up to take one last look. Just as he was pulling away, his eye caught a movement in the shadowed moonlight. A young Negro, probably in his late teens, was moving quietly across the lawns toward the woods. He was tall, and his muscles were already well developed from hard labor in the fields. The slave turned once and looked up at the house, but Gilly knew he hadn't been spotted in the dark window.

As the clouds parted again, a flood of moonlight illuminated the yard. The child had a clear view of the young buck's face. It was Cudjo, one of the new lot that Papa had purchased some months ago in Charleston. Two long, white scars ran diagonally down each of Cudjo's cheeks, and a bright band of copper hung about his neck. Gullah Jim had explained that the scars were marks of honor, given to Cudjo by his father when he still lived in Africa. The copper ring warded off sickness and evil.

Gilly knew that the African slave ships were illegal now. Laws had been passed to stop their offensive trade in human beings some years ago. The thousands upon thousands of Africans brought to America over the past two hundred years already far outnumbered their white masters here in the southern states, where slave labor was such a vital part of the economy.

But as young as he was, Gilly also knew that the trade still went on, albeit in secret. These very islands were ideal for such contraband activities. With their vast network of ocean inlets, rivers, and tidal creeks, the Sea Islands could swallow up a swift slaver as though it had never existed.

Cudjo was a product of that trade. He had come from Africa by way of the West Indies. He was strong and quick-witted, and by the time he was on the auction block in Charleston, he carried a chip of burning anger on his shoulder.

This was no way to treat the eldest son of an Ibo chieftain! Cudjo felt no pity for his fellow countrymen who were also being sold into slavery. They were beneath his station and worthy of their lot, but he had been destined to be a great chieftain. As the reality of his fall in status began to sink in, he determined that one day he would have his revenge.

Gilly watched Cudjo move toward the wood line and thought back to the day the young black had been brought to Coosaw by the overseer. The marks of the chains were still on his wrists and ankles, and the long, white scars on his face made him look as savage as any painted Indian. The overseer had obviously used force on the long journey home.

"Keep a sharp eye on that young buck," spit out the overseer as he discussed the latest purchases with Papa. "He's as mean as a crocodile and just about as uppity. Had to keep him chained the entire way down here. Sure wouldn't turn my back on him, not that one!"

Gilly had seen Cudjo look directly at the overseer then. He was too young to know what that look implied. A practiced observer, however, would have recognized it as pure hatred waiting only for the right time and place to erupt. Even Papa had missed it.

But as the months passed, young Cudjo settled into the routine of the plantation with surprising ease. His quick wits had often caught Gilbert Weldon's attention. The master saw the promise of leadership in the boy. If he failed to notice the calculating smile or the gleam in the eye, like that of a leopard waiting to pounce, it was only due to the fact that Cudjo had a way of worming himself into the master's good graces.

As the master's trust in him grew, Cudjo was given more and more responsibility, and with it a good deal more freedom. Perhaps that was why he was on his way into the forest on this particular night, though it was well past the curfew time, when the slaves were to remain in their quarters.

Gilly moved closer to the window as the last flickering shadows of Cudjo's figure disappeared into the underbrush. Again he heard the distant sound of the drums. Now he knew where Cudjo was going. He was going to the place of the drums!

2
Slave Cabin

The morning star was high in the eastern sky when the chanting began again. The drums were gone now, leaving in their wake the rhythmic sound of voices rising and falling with the wind. These voices held no threat for Gilly. He awakened to them every morning. Secure in his comfortable bed, he could allow the growing light to clear the fears of night from his mind. A new day awaited—its hours his to do with as he chose.

Not so for the slaves. Only the night was theirs. Before the first rays of sunlight touched the eastern horizon, they were roused from their quarters by the dissident clanging of the plantation bell. The dawn brought them no leisurely time for reflection. Still, with an optimism born of hope, they looked to the rising sun and called it "day clean"—a new day, a new beginning, one step closer to freedom.

The chanting grew louder. Gilly jumped from his bed and ran to the open window. The wide lawns were dark with shadows, but a faint glow of light touched the tops of the trees along the edge of the forest. As his gaze slid down the mass of dark trunks, a movement caught his eye. One tall black figure emerged from the shadows, then another, and another. They sang as they came and swayed in unison to the rhythm of the song.

Before long a single line of shuffling, swaying blacks was moving down the road that led from the woodland trail to the marshes. Over their shoulders the men carried hoes and shovels, while the women balanced wide baskets woven from grasses and reeds on top of their heads. Their bare feet thumped as they reached the firm mud of the high marsh. The morning breeze caught the words of their song and carried them to the boy standing at the window:

> We will all sing together on dat day,
> We will all sing together on dat day,
> An' I'll fall upon my knees
> An' face de risin' sun,
> Oh, Lawd, have mercy on me.

Gilly had his own name for the work that was to be done today. Mucking, that's what he called it, and he longed to run down to the marsh and join the people as they sloshed about in the thick mud. Each spring, marsh mud was collected and carried to the plowed fields. Then it was spread across the ground like chocolate icing on a cake. The thick mud, oxygen-poor but rich with decaying plant and animal matter, had the distinctive smell of rotten eggs. The sulphurous odor invaded the spring sweetness and mushroomed with intensity during the heat of summer, but its source brought life-giving fertility to the soil.

To Gilly's father, it was the smell of profit. "Take a good whiff, boy," he'd say with satisfaction. "Bad as it is, that odor is the promise of hard, cold cash!"

Gilly could see his father now. He was near the edge of the marsh, sitting astride his big roan horse. The master of Weldon Oaks sat tall and erect, looking every bit the prosperous planter. He had one knee slung casually across the saddle horn, with his wide-brimmed straw hat perched rakishly on his kneecap. The first rays of sunlight were turning the horizon golden pink, outlining the man and the horse with tinges of bronze, like a heroic statue.

The master was watching the long line of moving slaves. The boy, though he couldn't see it from this distance, was certain of the expression on his father's face. Pride, stern pride, the look of a man satisfied with his property.

Suddenly the master turned and looked up at his son's window. Wheeling the roan, Papa dug at his flanks with his heels and cantered across the lawn to the house.

"Well, boy, you gonna lounge about all day?" he shouted as he looked upward. "Rise and shine—there's work to be done!"

"But, Papa, I thought you said we'd go to the quarters first thing this morning. Don't you remember? We were going to get Maum Beezie."

"I said that *I* would go to the quarters. Don't recall including you in that plan, young man."

"Please, Papa. Please, may I go with you?"

"I might consider it if you get yourself down to breakfast within the next few minutes. Josephine has better things to do than wait half the morning for the likes of you."

Without further delay, Gilly tore across the floor to the heavy clothes press and pulled out a cotton shirt and a pair of trousers. He entered the dining room still struggling with his shirt buttons and failed to see the plump form of Josephine edging backward through the door. She was balancing a covered platter of food in one hand and a sweating pitcher of cold milk in the other. The tray tipped precariously as Gilly scuttled past her.

"Massa Gilly, you gib we a fright! Slow down, young-un, so's yo stomach can ketch up wid yo feet."

"Papa's waiting for me, Josephine. He's taking me to the quarters today!"

Josephine wrinkled her nose in distaste. "De quarters? Dat ain't no respectable place! What you wanna go der fer?" She lifted her chin and walked to the table with an air of superiority. House servants like Josephine considered themselves of a different breed and spoke of the slave quarters only in the most disparaging terms.

"We're going to get Maum Beezie. She'll be coming back to

the big house now."

Josephine's face softened at the sound of the old woman's name. "Well, now, dat's a different kettle ob fish!" Josephine placed the food on the table and pushed Gilly's chair under him. "Bout time too! De missus is plum wore out what wid a new baby comin'. Now set yo'self down an' eat." She started to walk from the room, then turned for one final warning. "And I reckin Maum Beezie kin handle de likes ob you. Hummpf! She ain't gwanna take no sass, and dat fer true." Straightening the bright red scarf that threatened to slip over one eye, the cook flounced her apron for emphasis and walked out the back door.

Gilly smiled at her back. How he loved Josephine! He had long since learned to ignore her uppity ways; they were just for show. Underneath her stained and flour-bespecked dress beat a heart of pure gold.

Within half an hour he was sitting on the front stairway waiting for Papa. The sun had worked itself over the horizon, and the air was growing warmer, although thin shadows still crept across the lawn. Gilly turned at the sound of hoofbeats and saw his father coming toward him astride the big roan. The animal pranced about nervously, fighting the bit and jerking at the reins. As good a rider as Papa was, he had to work to control the horse.

The animal reared when he reached the steps, his nostrils flaring and a wild look in his eyes. Gilly backed away, trying to keep a distance between himself and the massive horse; he feared this creature as he feared nothing else. Although no one would say it in front of Papa, Gilly knew the stable hands were also apprehensive about the animal. "Ho'se from de debil," they whispered under their breath, adding that he could have no more appropriate name.

Diablo sensed the boy's fear and began to prance sideways. He rolled his black eyes about until their whites showed like wide crescent moons. A long fleck of foam hung from the bit and flew through the air as the horse jerked back his head and blew loudly through his nostrils.

"Whoa there! Steady, Diablo." The horse reared as Papa tried to calm him. When he finally settled down, Papa threw his leg over the animal's flanks and slid easily out of the saddle. "Don't look so skittish, boy; Diablo won't eat you. A spirited horse is like a prime field hand; he has to be mastered. He needs to know who's in control. Showing fear is the worst thing you can do!" He brushed the dust from his hat and reached down, preparing to lift Gilly onto Diablo's broad back.

Gilly backed away again. "I . . . I'd rather walk, Papa."

"Walk! Now what kind of talk is that? It's high time you learned how to ride, boy."

"Papa, it isn't far to the quarters. Please. We can take the trail through the woods."

Gilbert Weldon looked angry but tied Diablo's reigns to the post. Wordlessly, he turned and walked with long strides toward the woods. His son was forced to run to keep up with him.

Papa was right, thought Gilly, as tears of guilt and shame pricked at the corners of his eyes. He'd have to learn how to ride someday. Though Coosaw was one of the smaller of the Sea Islands, it would be no easy job to walk its perimeter, and there wasn't another plantation on the whole island. Papa's fields stretched for miles across the flat landscape. The only other way to get about was by boat. In fact, Gilly thought, with a twinge of pleasure, a boat would be the perfect thing. Someday he would be the master of his own boat. Owning a boat would be better than owning a horse—better even than owning slaves.

Gilbert Weldon reached the beginning of the trail and turned to wait for his son. He slapped his riding crop against his leather boots impatiently. "Well, if you mean to walk, you'd best go at it with a bit more vigor, or you'll never get anywhere!"

Gilly plunged down the narrow path after the receding form of his father. There was a hard lump in his throat, and the palms of his hands felt sweaty. He should have gotten on that horse after all; then Papa wouldn't be angry with him. Why couldn't he ever seem to please his father?

The little tabby cabin of Maum Beezie was the first building of the slave quarters that they came to. It stood back in the woods, separated from the open area with its long rows of cabins facing each other in orderly precision. The other little cabins were also constructed of tabby because it was the most durable building material on the islands. Made of broken bits of oyster shell and the lime of burned shells, tabby withstood both the burning heat of summer and the onslaughts of cold winter storms with equal indifference. The remains of very old tabby walls still stood along the riverbank. No one was sure who had first built them or how long they'd been there.

Despite the similarities in building material, Maum Beezie's cabin had an independence that was apparent in the way it backed off into the woods, well apart from the general quarters. Above it rose the tall loblolly pines, whose roots grasped at the marshy woodland. The scaly cinnamon-colored bark on the trees blended with the red cedar clapboards of the cabin's roof. The front of the little dwelling boasted a doorway and one small, high window. There were no other windows in the structure. A rough chimney, also made of tabby, clung to the back wall. It, too, gave distinction to the dwelling. All of the other cabins had chimneys made of logs—a treacherous arrangement considering the fact that they caught fire on a regular basis.

Papa walked up to the rough-hewn wooden door and knocked politely. Under no circumstances would he ever pull rank on Maum Beezie. He respected her like he respected no other black on the entire plantation. It was she, after all, who had reared him.

Gilly felt the cool air of the interior even before he entered the door. The earthen floor, hard packed and shiny from years of footprints, was devoid of even the simplest of mattings. Maum Beezie didn't hold with such "fixin's." Reed mats, she insisted, bred insects and little "varmints."

Gilly scanned the one and only room of the building but saw no sign of the old Negro woman. "She's not here, Papa," he said, with disappointment in his voice.

"Most likely she's out gathering herbs. You sit down—and *don't* touch anything. I'll try to hunt her up."

Papa pushed Gilly down onto a small wooden stool and walked out the door, closing it shut behind him so that only the shaft of sunlight from the small window illuminated the cabin's interior. The child fidgeted about nervously. He'd never been in one of the slave dwellings before, and it made him feel decidedly uncomfortable. He pressed his hands into his lap and let his eyes adjust to the darkness.

The rest of the furnishings were as crude and simple as the little wooden stool. There was a table made of smoothed planks, an old rocking chair pulled up close to the fireplace, some slanting shelves built onto one of the walls, and, in the far corner, a double wooden bed. No thick, goose-down mattress rested on the taught ropes woven across the rough wooden frame. Rolled up at the foot of the bed was a thin mat filled with dried Spanish moss. One woolen blanket, dark with age and chimney smoke, hung neatly across the rolled mat.

But if the furnishings were without note, the objects scattered about the interior gave the cabin an entirely different dimension. Bundles of fragrant-smelling grasses hung from the ceiling rafters. Between the few bent pots and pans on the shelves lay an array of jars and bottles filled with mysterious-looking substances. Cut branches, drying leaves, and bits of roots were scattered on the tabletop. And from the red coals lying on the floor of the fireplace, a marvelous aroma drifted upward and tickled Gilly's nose.

The boy had all he could do to stay seated on the stool. He was just about to slip off and sidle over to the fireplace, when he heard the sound of Papa's voice approaching. Then the deep, rich laughter of the old woman filled the cabin.

"Me-oh-my, chil, you be de picture of yo papa when he ben small-small like de marsh rabbit!"

Gilly looked up into an ebony face creased with smile wrinkles. Dark eyes twinkled out at him, and a broad nose, as smooth and shiny as the wide cheeks, reflected the light streaming through the open doorway. The old woman's laughter bubbled up from her heavyset frame, and the chill of the cabin disappeared.

"Guess you ben a sniffin' my hoecakes. Time you sinks yo teeth into 'em."

She reached down and picked up a small rake that rested against the wall. Then scraping away the glowing coals, she slid a lovely little round cake from the ashes. She pulled a dented metal plate from the mantle shelf and scooped the cake up. Using the corners of her apron as hot pads, she picked up the cake, threw it from one hand to the other, and then brushed off the flaky white ashes. Putting the cake back onto the plate, she slid it under Gilly's chin.

Gilly breathed deeply of the delicious aroma before he bit into the edge of the hoecake. Steam rose up in a thin white line past his nose. The happy taste of sweet cornbread filled his mouth. He took large bites now, licking his lips with his tongue to catch the tiniest wayward crumb.

Papa sat down on an old wooden chair next to Gilly and looked longingly at the last bit of cornbread as it was stuffed quickly into his son's mouth.

"Now ain't dat sumpin," chuckled Maum Beezie as she walked back to the fireplace. "Dis here po' chil so hungry, he gobble up all dat hoecake afer he papa get eben a nibble!"

Again she sifted through the coals and raked out another fat little cake. This time she placed it before Master Weldon, grinning down on him with a pride fit to busting. Then she turned to Gilly and put her face close to his. "De secret ob my hoecakes," she whispered, "be in de wood. Good oak wood, dat what it take—make clean ash. Howsomeber, a li'l drop ob molasses don't hurt none."

Gilly and his father walked back along the wooded path in a far more amiable frame of mind. Master Weldon was feeling much better now, knowing that he could place everything in his old nurse's capable hands. Maum Beezie would be at the big house by tomorrow morning. There was the problem of Jeremiah, of course, but some sort of arrangements could be made. Turning to his son, the planter reached out and tousled the lad's hair affectionately.

Jeremiah was Maum Beezie's husband. He had served as the head groom on the plantation since he was just a young buck. No one could handle horses better than he. Even Diablo calmed under his touch. Gilbert Weldon, when he was just a boy about Gilly's age, had been taught to ride by Jeremiah.

The groom had started the young master on one of the little marsh tackies that roamed the islands, wild and free as their larger ancestors. They had originally been brought to the New World by the Spanish on their galleons. Many ships had floundered in the great hurricanes that swept this coast during the autumn months. Most of the men had been lost, but somehow a few of the horses had made it to the islands. After years of inbreeding, they had grown short and stocky, but they were still a gallant lot.

As they approached the open area around the house, Gilbert smiled at the memory of his first pony. Surely Gilly would be as pleased. He so wanted to get closer to his son. He reached back and lifted the boy onto his shoulders. "I've got a surprise for you, Gilly, something very special. Now I know you're not overly fond of Diablo. That's understandable; he's simply too big for you."

Gilbert could feel his son's body stiffen. The lad really was afraid! What ever could have caused that? Surely it wasn't that unfortunate accident with the young groom! The foolish buck had simply taken on more than he could handle when he thought to exercise Diablo that day. It was his own carelessness and poor riding skills that had brought about his death. Oh, well, all of Gilly's fear would disappear when he saw the lovely little marsh tacky he'd had Jeremiah bring in. Jeremiah had been breaking it for several days now, and it was as gentle as a lamb.

The old groom stood at the door of the stables waiting for them. He had a worried look on his face, but he tipped his hat respectfully when the master and his son approached. Cowering behind Jeremiah stood a young Negro boy about seven years of age. The child shuffled from one foot to the other, his eyes wide with fear.

Zach had come from Mount Hope, a plantation just north of Charleston. He knew that his former master had been too much of a gambler. He had lost a large sum of money and needed to make good on his debts. One day the overseer walked into the cabin where Zach lived with his mammy and two younger brothers. With hardly a word of explanation, Zach had been taken away. The next day he found himself standing on the auction block at the Charleston slave market. Within a week he had been brought down to Beaufort by steamer, and now he stood cowering at Jeremiah's side, waiting to meet his new master.

"Ah," said Gilbert as he spied the young black boy. "So he's come already. I wasn't expecting him today, but this will make the surprise all the better." He lifted Gilly off his shoulders. "Well, now it turns out that I have two surprises for you!"

Gilly looked cautiously at the black boy and wondered what other terror, beside riding lessons, lay in store. He watched his father step out and reach for the black child. Hunkering down, the master scrutinized his latest purchase.

"Fine-looking boy, Jeremiah. Open your mouth, lad, and let's have a look at your teeth. Hmm." He spun Zach around, inspecting him up and down as he would one of his animals. "Yes, I think you'll do just fine." Then he looked up at the old groom. "And what of the pony? Is he ready?"

Gilly felt confused. What did this black boy have to do with him getting a pony?

Jeremiah went into the stables and came out again leading a stocky little piebald pony with a coat of shaggy hairs and a long, rather disheveled mane. The animal was basically cream colored but sported a half-mask of black on his face and another large patch on his left rump. It gave him a comical look. Gilly felt the lump of fear in his stomach begin to melt. This funny little creature had no resemblance to Papa's big-muscled roan. The more he looked at the pony, the more he wanted to laugh.

Gilbert Weldon, however, did not look pleased. "I don't know, Jeremiah," he said, rubbing his chin. "This isn't exactly what I had in mind."

"Massa Weldon, suh, this here pony be bery good. Trust ol' Jeremiah. Ain't he always know what best? Ain't neber gwanna find a critter walkin' round on hoofs as fine as dis tacky." With that he turned and winked at Gilly.

Gilly walked up to the little pony and rubbed his neck. The tacky turned his head and nuzzled Gilly's hand affectionately. "I like him, Papa. I truly like him. I won't be afraid of riding now."

Papa rubbed his chin again and then turned to face the young black boy still cowering in the corner. "Step up here, Zach." He grasped Gilly's arm and pulled him in front of Zach. "I said that I have two surprises for you. I hope you like the second as well as the first. This here's Zach. I had the overseer buy him up in Charleston last week. He's your property now, son."

Gilly looked startled. "M-my property, sir?"

Jeremiah stepped forward and put his arm around Zach's trembling shoulders. "Berry well, den. Berry well. Massa Gilly, Zach gwanna be yo daily give servant. Gwanna take care ob you—polish yo shoes—set out yo clothes."

Then he turned to face Zach and chucked him under the chin. "And Zach gwanna be bery happy too. He ain't gwanna grow up to be no field niggra, no suh. Gwanna live in de big house an eat all dat good food what Josephine done cook. Yes, suh, de good Lawd look down on Zach and say, 'Looka dat fine boy. I es gwanna give dis boy to de nicest fambly in all de South.'"

Zach sniffled and swallowed hard, willing himself not to cry. He didn't want to live in that big house. He wanted to go back and live with Mammy and his little brothers in their own cabin. He tried not to remember the expression he had seen on Mammy's face that last day, when they had taken him away. He tried not to think about other times, good times, when she had held him in her arms and told him how much she loved him. But try as he might, the memory of her terror-filled eyes haunted him. Somewhere deep inside, he knew the truth. He would never see her again!

3
Wade in de Water

(1850)

Gilly awoke with a start. It was still dark in his room, but the thin light of early dawn flickered through the shutters. What had awakened him? Then he felt it, a presence, someone or—something! He could sense movement close by and a soft rhythmic noise. Was it the sound of breathing?

He searched the room with his eyes. Nothing. He held his breath and listened. Had something come through the window last night? He'd been told that the night air was dangerous; it carried fevers and disease. But perhaps there were even greater dangers—unseen things prowling about in the darkness, searching for open windows.

He thought of the slaves' tales of witchcraft. Were they only tales? Josephine believed them. She sprinkled salt on her bed each evening before going to sleep. Once, in play, he had hidden her saltshaker, but the cook had turned on him, her eyes wild with fright. "Please, Massa Gilly, don't neber mobe dat salt in de night."

"Why?" he had asked, seeing that her fear was real.

"I's scared to death ob de hag."

"The hag? What's a hag, Josephine?"

"Dat be de witch, de plat-eye. Come in de dark—through de window—mayhap right through de keyhole. Look just like a black cat, eyes ob fire an' tail switchin' like de water moccasin. She hiss an' spit; den she come at you. Ride you till you hardly ken ketch your breaf. No-o, Massa Gilly, I don't get no sleep worryin' 'bout dat hag slippen' into my room."

"But why do you sprinkle salt around?" asked Gilly.

Josephine rolled her eyes, her face still a mask of fear. "Salt be de best way to keep she out. Hags neber come near my bed effen it sprinkle wid salt. Some folks puts de broom 'cross dey door, but I allows dat salt be de best."

Gilly went to his mother with the story. "Oh, child, you mustn't pay any attention to these superstitions," she said firmly. "They're nothing but tales. There are no such things as hags or witches or plat-eyes."

"But there *are* conjure doctors, Mama. Even Gullah Jim says so. He told me of an old Negro who lives deep in the woods on St. Helena's Island—and he's a conjure doctor, for sure. He puts voodoo spells on people and everything."

Mama lifted him up onto her lap and looked straight into his eyes. "Gilly, listen to me carefully. Gullah Jim is right. There are people who practice voodoo and witchcraft, but such things are evil, and you must stay away from them. Conjure doctors and voodoo spells are dangerous; there's a power behind them—a satanic power."

Gilly was shocked. "But, Mama, if those things are evil, then Josephine must be evil too!"

"Oh, no!" said Mama. "Josephine's not evil; she's just superstitious. You see, she was taught to be fearful of these things by her parents, and they, in turn, were taught the same fears by their parents. Superstitions, son, are carried down from one generation to another."

"But why do the conjure doctors do such things?" asked Gilly.

Marian Weldon thought for a long moment. "Well, son," she began, "I guess it's a way to have power over other people's lives. Someone with evil power uses superstition and fear. Voodoo and conjuring are ways to keep people frightened in order to have power over them. That's what I mean about it being dangerous. You must never let an evil person have power over your life."

Gilly nodded; then his face brightened. "Gullah Jim says it's all tricks anyway."

"Yes," answered Mama, "much of it is just trickery, but when you're frightened, your mind can play tricks on you. You begin to see and hear things that aren't really there."

Thinking back to that conversation he had had with his mother, Gilly began to feel better. Perhaps his mind was just playing tricks on him. Maybe there was nothing in the room after all. But just to be sure, he slid down and pulled the covers over his head.

Everything was very quiet. Then, from somewhere nearby, he thought he heard a scratching noise. Lifting the covers, Gilly listened intently. The noise seemed to be coming from under his bed. He held his breath. The bed started to shake, and the scratching noise grew louder. Suddenly his mattress gave a mighty lurch. Gilly let out a scream and ducked under the covers. A shrill echo of his cry came from under the bed. It sounded distinctly human.

Throwing back the covers, Gilly rolled over to look down at the floor. A foot struck him in the face. He pulled back in alarm and examined the offensive object. There were two of them, both black, the soles caked with mud. Thankfully the feet were attached to legs. The rest of the body, if there was one, was concealed by the bed.

"Hey, get out from under my bed!" he shouted, his fear momentarily overcome by anger.

The feet and legs began to wriggle, and gradually the body emerged. It was small and thin, covered with ragged clothes. Then a wooly black head with two startled eyes popped up. The face belonged to Zach.

Now Gilly was angry. "What are you doin' under my bed?" he shouted. "Did you sleep under there?"

Zach sat on his knees and touched his hand to his forehead. "No, massa. I jes come."

"For what?"

"For de bucket."

"The bucket?" asked Gilly in surprise. "What bucket?"

"Chamber bucket, suh. De missus tell we to collect he."

"It's not a bucket; it's a pot," Gilly corrected. "It's called a chamber pot."

"Yes, suh, same thing. Where he be?"

Gilly sighed. He dropped his chin into his hands and gave Zach a withering look. "I don't keep it under my bed."

"Where he be, den?"

"In the closet. If you must know, I keep it in the closet."

Zach looked startled. "Dat ain't no place fer de chamber bucket . . ." then, remembering his place, he quickly added, "massa, suh."

"Well, it's *my* place for it! Besides, I don't like people crawling around my room while I'm asleep." Gilly jumped out of bed and stomped toward the clothes press. To his dismay, he found his shirt and pants hanging neatly over the back of a chair. He scowled at them. "What are my clothes doing there?"

"Waitin' for you to gets in 'em, suh."

Gilly kicked the chair, and the clothes went sprawling across the floor. "Stop calling me sir! My name is Gilly."

"Yes, Massa Gilly, suh."

The young master lunged at the black boy and grabbed the front of his ragged shirt. "I don't know why Papa bought you. You're impossible! Look at your clothes, they're a ragged mess! And your feet are even worse; there's mud all over them! You don't belong in the big house—you belong in the fields!"

Zach's chin began to tremble, and his eyes grew large with fright. "Please, Massa Gilly, de missus whup me effen I don' call you suh. I is just tryin' to do what she say."

Gilly looked down at the trembling boy. He hadn't really meant to scare him so. Of course, Mama wouldn't whip him. Where had he gotten such an idea? Then he remembered what Mama had said about using fear to have power over other people's lives. That kind of power was evil, she had said. Gilly began to feel uncomfortable. He reached down and touched the boy's shoulder. "Oh, come on, then," he said brusquely, "I don't want to be late. Gullah Jim is taking me fishing in his boat. If you promise not to get in the way, we might consider taking you too."

Zach grabbed up the pot and raced to do his chore. Gilly was ready to go by the time he returned. With a curt nod, the young master headed out the door. He took the stairs two at a time, Zach close at his heels. At the landing Gilly pulled up short and spun around, but Zach couldn't stop in time. He skidded into the white boy with such force that the two of them nearly took a tumble.

"I said not to get in my way," yelled Gilly. "I don't like to be shadowed. Stay back, yuh hear me?"

Zach backed away. "Yes, suh, Massa Gilly."

"And what did I tell you about calling me sir?"

Gilly had his fists raised ready to strike, when a deep voice from the bottom of the stairs stopped him cold. "If anyone gwanna do de whuppin', it gwanna be me."

Gilly spun around. Maum Beezie, hands planted firmly on her hips, stood looking up at him. He had forgotten that she was coming this morning.

The old woman examined him critically. "Don't see no shoes," she said, her voice carrying the unmistakable ring of authority. "Now you march yo'self back up dem stairs an' gets 'em fast."

"Don't need shoes," answered Gilly sullenly. "I'm going fishing with Gullah Jim. Fishermen never wear shoes!"

"Fishermans hab tough skin on de bottom ob dey feets. Yo skin be soft—soft like de belly ob de frog!"

Zach tried to hold back a laugh, but it came out as a half-burp, half-giggle. Gilly swung on him again, but Maum Beezie grabbed his arm in midair.

"Maum Beezie don't stand for chilluns catawallin' in de stairwell. Now, Massa Gilly, if you wants ta go fishin', you best find yo shoes, likity-split."

Turning reluctantly, Gilly started back up the steps. He knew he'd met his match.

Maum Beezie waited until the young master was gone, then turned to Zach. "Chil'." She smiled at him kindly. "A boy what's gwanna work in de big house need better clothes on he back an' shoes fer he feet. When you done wid de fishin', we is gwanna finds you somepin proper to wear, and dat for true!" She stretched her arms out to him, and Zach fell into their warm embrace. The tears he'd held back yesterday came freely now.

The sun was cresting the horizon when the boys reached the river's edge. Gullah Jim was already there, busily mending a net. He sat cross-legged on the dock near his small sailboat, with the tattered net spread across his legs. He glanced up at Gilly and smiled a welcome, and then tipped his high-topped beaver hat respectfully. The poor old hat had seen better days. Its brim was torn and ragged, and its top badly dented, but Jim never went fishing without it. The dented top made a perfect platform upon which he could balance his fishing bucket.

The old man's grizzled hair, peppered with silver, stuck out in tufts from under his hat. His face was thin and lined, his skin wrinkled and thick like old leather. A permanent squint pulled at the corners of his eyes as though he was always looking into the sun, but the lines of his face rarely held a scowl. As far as Jim was concerned, there was very little in life worth scowling over.

Though he was a slave, Gullah Jim had the face of a man who knew what it was to roam freely over the earth. His skills as a fisherman had won him that right, and not even the master questioned his comings and goings. He spent his days exploring the tidal rivers and creeks or wandering through the marshes and woodlands. On many occasions he had taken his sturdy little craft well beyond the bays and inlets surrounding the islands and ventured out into the open ocean itself.

Gullah Jim was anxious to be underway now. There was a bit of weather brewing to the north, and the water in the sound would be choppy. The tide was going out, and the receding river had left the prow of his boat resting in thick mud. He directed the boys to walk down to the end of the dock; then he stepped into the shallows and began working the boat backward, lifting and pushing it with his strong, wiry arms.

Gilly sat impatiently on the edge of the dock. He looked at his shoes. They were entirely out of place—besides, they pinched his toes. Why had Maum Beezie been so insistent that he wear them? Zach wasn't wearing shoes. He glanced down at Jim's legs. The old man's feet had sunk deeply into the sticky mud. Obviously Jim's feet were bare too. Well, he wasn't about to look like a landlubber. Jumping up, he kicked off his shoes and shoved them under a pile of nets.

Within minutes the boat was floating free, and Jim motioned for the boys to hop in. Gilly, anxious to be underway, was quick to respond, but Zach stood back hesitantly. He had done a lot of fishing in his day, but always from solid ground. Jim climbed onto the deck and held out his hand to the boy. Helping him into the boat, he patted him reassuringly on the back. "Ki!" he said with a broad grin. "You be a fishermans if ever I seen 'em!"

Zach grinned and nodded. He edged forward, drawn by the old man's confident smile. The boat began to sway, and he grasped nervously for the boom, not realizing that, if not secured, it could easily swing out and throw him overboard. Again the fisherman was there, holding him steady and helping him find his footing. The rocking boat made Zach nervous; he began to tremble. Should he tell Mister Jim that he couldn't swim? No, not in front of Gilly. The young master thought so little of him as it was.

Jim sensed the boy's fear. He also felt the thinness of the small arm through the ragged shirt sleeve. The old man's heart gave a lurch. There was something about this youngster that reminded him of his own son. Where was his boy now? Of course, he would be a grown man if he were still alive. For all of Jim's happy-go-lucky attitude, the thought of his lost son weighed heavily on his heart. Having no desire to be a fisherman like his father and rebelling at even the thought of slavery, the boy had bolted when he was in his teens. Had he made it to safety? Jim would never know, but it was best not to wonder about such things. In fact, he had almost forgotten until now, but seeing this boy brought them back—the old memories and feelings that he thought had long since gone.

With the two boys seated comfortably at the bow and Jim positioned at the stern so he was free to work both the tiller and sail, the little bateau headed out onto the Coosaw River. There was a stiff breeze from the northwest. The spritsail quivered in the wind and then billowed out. With a sudden lurch, the sailboat keeled over, then raced before the wind. It swung quickly around the tip of Morgan Island and onto the wide backwaters of St. Helena Sound.

Jim kept a careful watch on the sky to the northeast. A distant gray sheet of rain hung like a veil, obscuring the southern tip of Edisto Island. The cloud was moving rapidly. It soon cleared the island and moved over the open waters of the sound. The boat was close enough so the boys could see the heavy sheets of rain flattening the waves at the estuary's mouth. As they sailed swiftly to the open water, the waves turned into long rollers that moved relentlessly inward, with a head of white foam gathering at their curling crests.

Jim nosed his craft diagonally toward the oncoming rollers. As the boat cut neatly through them, a heavy salt spray flew across the bow, thoroughly soaking the two young fishermen. The waves grew steadily larger, and the boat rose high over each crest and then fell with a jolting thud, only to be lifted again by the next wave. The foaming water gurgled under the hull, and the rising wind lashed it over the gunwales in sheets of spray.

Jim broke his concentration from the movement of the waves to glance toward the bow. He worried that the rough seas were too much for the boys. Perhaps he shouldn't be taking them this far out. One look at Gilly's face, however, set him at ease. The boy was transfixed with happiness. He had found his element. Jim understood the look immediately and knew that a seaman had been born.

Gilly noticed Jim looking at him and raised his arm in mock salute. The timing was poor. Caught at the top of a wave, he was lifted clean off his seat as the small boat plunged over the crest and dropped into the deep trough behind it. Nonplused, Gilly let out a wild shout of joy.

Zach, on the other hand, was considerably more subdued. He tried to act brave, but his eyes showed fear. He grasped at the gunwales for dear life. With each wild lift and fall of the boat, he made an effort to stay planted firmly on the seat. It was, of course, impossible under the circumstances—like trying to stay in the saddle of a bucking horse. Jim called to him, urging him to ride with the movement, but his words were blown away by the heavy wind.

He decided it was time to work the boat closer to the protective shoreline. Steering a course for south-southeast, Jim calculated that he would soon have to alter direction to clear the wide sandbanks lying off the northern tip of Hunting Island. The shallower waters around the small barrier island's northern perimeter were his favorite fishing grounds.

Zach looked more relaxed as they moved out of the heavy surf and into the eddying waters around the sandbanks. Spotting a length of twine coiled about a small stick, the boy picked it up and tied on a hook and sinker, and then neatly attached the bait. Gilly watched as Zach dropped the line into the water.

Gullah Jim, in the meantime, had retrieved his hand-woven cast net from the bottom of the boat. Maneuvering close to a high sandbar, he dropped anchor. "Gwanna get we some bait fish," he said simply.

Little flat islands of wet sand were gradually being exposed to the sunlight as the receding tide pulled the waters of the bay seaward. Between the small islands, however, were deep holes and gullies where small fish found themselves trapped by the dropping water. Jim waded along the edges of the sandbars and scanned the deeper depressions. It wasn't long before he motioned for Gilly and Zach to join him.

Still apprehensive, Zach pointed down to his line. He was quite content to stay right where he was. Gilly, on the other hand, was anxious to learn all he could about the art of fishing. He rolled up his pant legs and slid over the side into the cool, swirling waters of the bay. How thankful he was that he had left his shoes behind!

Jim was preparing his folded net. Placing the center of it between his teeth, he grasped the drawstring with one hand and the weighted edges with the other. Gilly stood back to give him room but watched the old man closely. Winding his arm for the throw, Jim cast the net out in a wide arc. It landed in the water with a clean splash, and as he drew it backward, the water fairly boiled with little silver fish that flashed and wriggled in the sunshine. The net was heavy with them.

Gilly was fascinated. It had looked so easy. He wished he could try his hand with the net but said nothing. There were more basic things to be learned first. Perhaps he should try his hand at fishing with a simple hook and line like Zach was doing. He waded back to the boat and was amazed to find that the black boy had already caught two good-sized fish. A warm smile creased Zach's face as he offered his line to Gilly.

Within minutes of dropping the line in the water, Gilly felt a sharp tug. He jerked his arm up so swiftly that the hook flashed above the surface. It was picked clean of bait! Disappointed, he let Zach rebait the hook. Then he once more dropped the line over the side. This time, when the nibble came, he was more cautious. He waited, like he'd seen Zach do, until the tugging became persistent. Then slowly, cautiously, keeping the line taut, he rolled the string around the stick, pulling in the hook. To his dismay, the bright blue claw of a crab broke the surface of the water. But before he could bring it in, the crab dropped off the line and disappeared into the stirred-up mud beneath the boat.

Zach looked at Gilly and smiled. "Massa Gilly, suh, is you catchin' crabs, or is you catchin' fish?"

"I'm not *catching* anything!" said Gilly testily.

Gullah Jim, amused by the conversation, listened to the boys. There was a tone in Zach's voice that made him decide not to interfere.

"Well, suh," continued Zach, "if you be catchin' crab, den

you droppin' yo line jes right. But if you be catchin' fish, dat calls for sumpin' else."

Gilly glanced at Zach warily. "Something else?"

Zach reached for his young master's line. "You droppin' de bait into de mud. Dat be right where ol' brudder crab lib. He see dat nice li'l fish wrigglin' round in de mud, he say, 'Yas suh, dat ma dinna fo' true.' Den he nip off li'l fish an' go home to feed his chilluns."

Gilly grinned crookedly at Zach.

"Now, suh," continued the black boy, "effen it be fish you after, you gotta hold dat line up out ob de mud. Hang he right below de surface—wiggle he round now and den. Purty soon big fish come along. See li'l fish playin' in de sunshine an' say, 'I es gwanna take dat silly li'l fish home an' feed my chilluns.' An' dat be jes what he do. Only afore he starts ta commence, you pull he in. Den *you* be de one who take both li'l fish an' big fish home for dinna."

Gilly's face broke into a wide smile. "Sure enough, Zach! I bet you're right."

Zach reached into the bait bucket and lifted out another wriggling little fish. He handed it to Gilly confidently. Gilly reached for it, but the slippery little creature flipped out of his hand and fell back into the water. Gilly shrugged and handed his line to Zach. Gilly watched closely as the black boy skillfully slipped the bait fish onto the hook.

"Ain't hard," said Zach.

Gilly smiled and nodded. "I'll be able to do it next time."

"Sho nuff, suh."

"Zach," Gilly said quietly, "if you call me Gilly, we can be friends."

"Dat for true?" asked Zach. Gilly nodded. "All right, den," Zach added. "When we fishin', I call you Gilly. But when yo mama an' papa be round, I calls you Massa Gilly, suh."

Jim climbed back into the boat and winked at Zach. The boy had jaw sense, all right. The times would be seldom when he could safely speak his mind in front of the buckra, as the Gullah people called the whites. But when in the presence of the real master and mistress, he must always say only that which they wanted to hear.

It was late afternoon by the time the little boat headed for home. The catch had been good, and Jim was content to know that in the slave quarters, as well as in the big house, a good fish dinner would be served at night.

The boys were in a talkative mood. Gilly told Zach of the Indians who had lived on these islands when his great-grandfather first came to settle the land and built what would become a successful plantation. He spoke of his family with obvious pride.

Zach, not to be outdone, now took up the conversation. He told Gilly that his father had been a driver on the plantation where Zach had been born. He was much respected by his people. Things would have continued to go well if the master hadn't taken up gambling. Actually, it was the other way around—the gambling took him! He played too often and lost too much. As the debts increased, so did the master's mistreatment of his slaves.

Zach spoke proudly of how his father tried to protect the people under his leadership, but things just went from bad to worse. Zach's papa had to stick his neck out too many times. It wasn't long before the master started to turn his violence on the driver.

"My pappy don't like de goins on," said Zach slowly. "One day he say, 'I is gwanna talk wid de massa.' An' dat be de last we eber see ob Pappy." Zach's eyes grew misty as he continued. "He jes neber come back. Some say de massa sell he off, an' some say he jes start to run and keep goin'. But de ol' folks, those what come from Africa, dey jes smile an' say, 'He ben one ob de special folk. He ben one what finally learn ta fly. He fly so high, an' he fly so far, dat one day he jes lift off an' fly right back ta Africa!' "

Gilly sat up in the boat and looked at Zach with startled eyes. Then he turned questioningly to Gullah Jim. "Is that possible, Jim? Is it possible that a person can fly?"

Jim was silent for a long time. When he finally spoke, he looked straight at Zach instead of Gilly. "Hmm, I hab heard dat sort ob story many time, many time fer true. Can't say effen a person can fly, 'cause I ain't neber seen no flyin' peoples. But I do thinks dis—effen de Lawd look down, and He see some poor soul what ben suffrin' an' worryin' ober udder folks more den he ben worryin' ober heself, den de Lawd sho gwanna mark 'em out as special."

As the little boat drifted slowly back toward the plantation grounds, the singing of the slaves trudging home from their hard day in the fields floated over the now-gentle waters of the river. Jim's eyes misted over with tears as he listened to the simple words:

> I work hard in de fields all day.
> I t'ank God day is done.
> But I'm neber too tired fer ta pray.
> I t'ank God day is done.

As the familiar verse continued, Jim lifted his lined face toward the darkening skies and sang with his people:

> E'er I get to dat mountaintop
> I t'ank God day is done.
> I praise my God an' neber stop.
> I t'ank God day is done.

The boat bumped quietly against the dock. Jim looked down at the two young boys and saw that they were sleeping peacefully. A lovely thought suddenly came to his mind. Perhaps, just as there were different ways of learning to fish and different ways to build a friendship, there were also different ways of learning to fly. Perhaps, even though a person's body was mired down in the fields of slavery, his mind could still be free to fly to a better place and a better time.

Jim retrieved Gilly's shoes from under the fishing nets before lifting the sleeping child and carrying him to the big house. No point in raising Maum Beezie's dander. She was waiting for them, scowling deeply when she saw the young master's bare feet. "Tain't fittin'!" she said reprovingly. "Dis boy ain't no fishermans."

Jim grinned at her. "Now, Beezie," he said, with an indulgent smile. "Usins had some wadin' ta do. Shoes ain't made fo' wadin'."

Clucking her tongue, the black woman pointed to the stairway. She'd see to it that Gilly got some supper later, but right now he needed to sleep. "Tain't fittin'," she muttered under her breath. "He papa not gwanna like it. Dis boy born ta be massa, not fishermans." She tucked him into bed and shook her head worriedly. There would be rough waters ahead for Gilly and his father.

Jim returned to the boat for Zach. The black boy was sound asleep in the bow, his head resting on a rolled net. As Jim looked down at the child's face, soft and vulnerable now in sleep, the memories of his own son flooded back. With great tenderness the old man lifted Zach and carried him to his little shanty by the side of the river. Placing the boy in his own bed, Jim nodded with satisfaction. "Mayhap some day, boy," he whispered, "you learn how ta fly too!"

4
The Sorcerer

(1850)

Thin shavings, as translucent as parchment, flew from the long stick as the knife blade flashed in the sun. Cudjo's slender fingers moved over the wood, feeling for its grain, turning and twisting it with the precision of an artist. Gradually the shape of a coiled snake emerged, as though it had been there all along, waiting only for a master carver to bring it to life. Its head, poised as though ready to strike, formed the knob at the top, while its sinuous body lay in graceful curves down and around the tapering rod.

Zach's eyes grew large with wonder. He had never seen such beautiful carving as Cudjo could do. In his pocket lay a small figure of a frog, every detail perfect, even down to the protruding tongue and bulbous toes. Cudjo had carved it for him just the day before.

"I heard tell ob dat rod he be makin'," whispered Zach to Gilly, afraid to break the concentration of the carver. "Dat be de rod ob Moses what led de chillun ob Israel out from Egypt."

Gilly nodded, too awestruck to answer. He dearly hoped that Cudjo would do a carving for him but didn't have the courage to ask. He was almost afraid to ask. Why? What was there about this black man that set him apart from the other slaves? Not even the house servants held the same fascination. A special strength, perhaps? No, more like a power.

Gilly watched Cudjo's movements. Nothing was wasted. Every action was calculated, refined, and meant to impress. He held himself erect when he walked, not slouched and bent in the menial posture of a field hand. His head had a nobility to it, the features of his face as finely carved as the figurines he produced with such artistry. His arms and legs, though muscular, were long and well-formed, tapering to hands and fingers beautiful in their symmetry. Even his speech, still rich with the distinctive accent of his mother tongue, was above that of his fellow slaves. Cudjo had an ear for language. He had picked up the English spoken by his masters in a very short time.

Zach was still whispering about Moses and the wonderful rod that had turned into a snake. Gilly wondered momentarily where the black boy had heard the story. Certainly not in the plantation chapel. The itinerant preachers who made the circuit of these island plantations knew better than to fill the slaves' heads with stories of liberation and freedom. Their sermons were always carefully constructed around texts that admonished obedience and willing servitude.

Cudjo held the finished rod up for inspection and then pointed it directly at Zach. His mouth turned up into a sarcastic grin. Then he began to laugh, slowly at first, the sound filled with mockery and coming from deep within his throat. "Poor little Zach. The slave boy." With a sudden slashing movement, he whipped the tapered end of the rod across Zach's face, leaving a long red welt on the child's left cheek. "Filled you with their lies, haven't they, boy?"

Zach fell back, wincing with pain, its cause not so much the sting of the rod as the mocking, penetrating voice that mercilessly lashed out at him. The truth of Cudjo's words burned into his brain. Once again he saw his mother's stricken face as he was pulled from her arms. The mark on his face would fade, but the memory of those words would haunt him like a recurring nightmare.

Taking sadistic delight in the pain he had caused, Cudjo tilted back his head and laughed with wild abandon. When he at last brought himself under control, he reached out and touched the welt on Zach's cheek as though it were, like the scars on his own face, a mark of honor. Lifting the rod to his chest, he rubbed his hand along the coiled form of the snake, gently caressing the smooth wood.

"No, boy," said Cudjo, his voice low and controlled, "this ain't the rod of Moses. It won't set you free. You need another rod for that—a magician's rod—a conjure rod!"

Then, as suddenly as before, his countenance changed again. His eyes flashed with an inner fire. "The power of Poro has caught you, boy!" he shouted.

Cudjo threw the carved stick into the air. It spiraled upward and then flipped over, the knobbed end coming down first. It fell with a hard thud at the crest of a low hill, the impact sending up a cloud of dust, obscuring the boys' vision. When the dust subsided, the rod was gone. Gilly and Zach ran to the top of the hill in time to see a twisting movement as the rod rolled to the bottom and disappeared under a bush.

Cudjo was still laughing, but there was no joy in the sound. It was ominous, threatening, filled with a strange darkness. He turned to Gilly, his face sober, his eyes burning into the white boy's in a way that seemed to hold him captive. "Put out your hand," he commanded.

Gilly was terrified by what he had witnessed. Without thinking, he put out his hand. Cudjo pressed a small, hard object into it. It was the carving of a man. Turning it over, Gilly examined the features. How strange! It looked like the face of the overseer.

"Keep it; it's yours for now. No one else must see it. When the time's right, I'll come and get it. Do you understand me, buckra boy?"

Gilly didn't understand but was too frightened to do anything more than nod in agreement. Grasping the coarse wood of the figurine with his fingertips, he pushed it down into his pocket. It felt heavy there, as though it didn't belong. Why hadn't Cudjo made him a frog as he had for Zach, or perhaps another animal—maybe a pony like Nutmeg? There was something all wrong, something terribly frightening about this man-image.

Without another word, Cudjo turned his back and walked away. The boys stood at the top of the hill, staring at the young black man as he disappeared over the knoll. Then they faced each other, turned in unison, and scrambled down to the bottom of the hill. But search as they might, they could find nothing of the carved rod with its coiled snake.

"Dat Cudjo be no good," warned Zach. "He got bad magic—voodoo magic! I hear tell dat Cudjo's pappy back in Africa ben a sorcerer. Mayhap Cudjo be one too. Listen, Gilly, you chuck dat t'ing away what he done carved fer you. You heist he up an' chuck he as far as you can."

Gilly hesitated, then shook his head. "Naw, it's all just a trick. He's trying to scare us." He paused. "Well, he doesn't scare me!" Taking the little figurine out of his pocket, he examined it again. "It's nothing but a carved piece of wood. What's so bad about an old piece of wood, anyway? Shucks, it doesn't scare me none." He put the carving back in his pocket, turned, and walked away.

Zach reached up and gingerly touched the stinging scar on his cheek. Why was his young master so blind? He shook his head in wonder. Gilly just didn't understand the dangers of voodoo magic. He had tried to warn him. What else could he do? Shrugging his shoulders, he pulled the carved frog from his pocket and threw it as far away as he could. Without even watching where it landed, he turned and ran down the trail after the disappearing form of Gilly.

The days passed, and Gilly soon forgot about the little carving of the man. He had kept it in his pocket for at least a week, then tucked it away in a box and placed it for safekeeping on a high shelf in his bedroom closet. Cudjo had probably just been joshing about wanting it back again. Several times he was on the verge of asking Zach to explain its meaning, but then he thought better of it. The black boy was too superstitious and obviously frightened to death by all this talk of voodoo. Besides, Gilly really *did* want to keep the carving, black magic or not.

But he was totally unprepared for his next meeting with Cudjo.

It was a cool day in early December, and he felt the urge to be away from the house. Mama had been in a tizzy for days. With the holidays coming and her pregnancy advancing, she'd been fussing at the house servants almost constantly. Nothing would please her but that the whole place be turned upside down and pulled inside out. She complained that the servants were lazy, and, for some unknown reason, she had come down especially hard on Zach. Josephine, sizing up the problem in her own inimitable way, had finally put Zach to work cleaning the outside kitchen house.

Gilly managed to corner his young servant when Josephine wasn't looking and got the boy to slip him a piece of fresh gingerbread that had been set out to cool.

"Let's take Nutmeg out for a ride, Zach. We'll go to the Morgan River and play Indians. No one'll ever catch us there."

Zach rolled his eyes and shook his head. "Um-mm, no suh! Ain't figurin' on gettin my hide tanned! Yo mammie got a bee in she bonnet fer certain. Tain't gwanna be dis boy what cross she path, no how!"

Gilly stifled his anger. Zach was right. The two of them had gotten into nothing but trouble lately. The best thing to do was just lie low and wait until the storm clouds passed over.

Stuffing the last bits of warm gingerbread into his mouth, he shrugged his shoulders, nodded at Zach, and walked away. He made a wide circle of the house and headed for the stables. Jeremiah was nowhere in sight. That was just as well; the old groom asked too many questions anyhow. He went to the tack room to get Nutmeg's saddle and bridle. No one was there, either. It didn't matter; he could do the job himself.

Within minutes the boy and his mount were making their way toward the narrow trail that ran through the deeply wooded southwestern end of the island. The air was crisp and cool. Nutmeg, glad to stretch his muscles and feel the soft earth of the trail beneath his hooves again, readily set up a brisk trot. As for Gilly, the exhilaration of being on his own, free from the hustle and bustle of the house, filled him with a sense of adventure.

Only one thing caused a small bit of worry in his mind. When he saddled Nutmeg, he noticed that one of the cart horses was missing from her stall, but the cart itself was still standing in its usual place under the stable overhang. Perhaps Jeremiah had gone on an errand for Papa. If that were the case, his best bet would be to stay well clear of any main trails. Jeremiah didn't like Gilly riding off by himself, and if the old groom spotted him, he'd most likely want to know where he was going.

The fact was, Gilly didn't have any definite plans. He just wanted to roam, to do some exploring. Perhaps he could search for tracks and signs like the Indians did. Or he could make believe that he was hunting for some great, wild creature of the wilderness—perhaps a bear or a cougar. Yes, that was it, he'd search for bear tracks.

The swells of firm ground gradually gave way to marshy areas, where the muddy trail clearly defined the prints of even the smallest of animals. Gilly hadn't gone more than a few feet over such terrain when he spotted the distinctive hoof marks of a shod horse. Reigning in Nutmeg, he slid from the saddle and examined the prints more closely. They were fresh, made scarcely an hour ago, with no overlying marks of birds or the little creatures that constantly scurried across this trail. And they were wide, like the hooves of the cart horse. Odd, thought Gilly. Why would Jeremiah come back here? This trail led nowhere in particular; as a matter of fact, it tended to simply peter out into the swampy woodland that lay along the banks of the Morgan River. Being very particular about the horses under his care, Jeremiah would hardly like them ridden into an area that might be the hiding places of venomous creatures like diamond-backed rattlers or cotton-mouths.

Now his curiosity was aroused. He climbed back into the

saddle and followed the markings of the earlier rider, feeling pleased at his ability to read the signs so clearly. There was, however, something strange about this trail. Gilly felt certain that, whoever was on the cart horse, it was *not* Jeremiah. There was an erratic pattern to the prints, as though the rider were inexperienced, or the horse had been agitated and nervous.

That thought slowed him down and took a good deal of the pleasure out of his little adventure. Several times he thought of turning back, but then berated himself for the idea. An Indian wouldn't be frightened by the thought of another rider in the forest. Patting Nutmeg's neck reassuringly, he pushed on. He could feel the tension in the little tacky's movements; he, too, was nervous.

Now a new idea began to assert itself, and try as he might, he couldn't shake it. He had the definite sensation that some real danger lay ahead. All thoughts of playing at Indians vanished. Not even the wild animals of the swampy woodlands held the threat that this new fear gave him. Without willing them, snatched bits of memories about voodoo and witchcraft came into his mind. Yet why he should be thinking of such things now, he couldn't imagine.

The trail was growing narrower, and the floor of the pine woodland was choked with thick growths of scrub palmetto and sharp, twisting vines. Sliding down from Nutmeg, Gilly decided to walk the little pony so as not to blunder into a dead fall of tree limbs. The ground, carpeted as it was by a thick layer of pine straw, muffled the sounds of the animal's hoofbeats. Only the occasional crack of a breaking branch told of their presence in the woods.

Then, at the top of a rise, he caught the whiff of wood smoke. He stopped short and scanned the lower land ahead of him. Was the smoke coming from that grove of live oaks ahead? He thought he detected a haziness between the massive trunks and twisted, low-hanging branches. Long shrouds of swaying Spanish moss obstructed the rest of his view, but it was very possible that someone had a campfire in the grove.

He studied the trail at the bottom of the ridge. Yes, the hoof prints were clearly defined in the soft earth; a rider had recently passed that way. Once again the tingling sensation of impending danger warned him to turn back.

And he might have, but before he could make his decision, his ears caught a strange sound. Turning his head to listen better, his eyes suddenly grew wide with amazement. It was chanting that he heard, and it came from the grove. There was no way he could control his curiosity now. Wrapping Nutmeg's reins around a tree trunk, he made his way cautiously forward, stopping frequently to scan the terrain ahead.

The chanting grew louder as he approached the oaks, and added to the smell of wood smoke was another, more pungent odor. At first it reminded him of the rotten-egg smell of marsh mud, but added to it was a cloying sort of sweetness that grew more overpowering as he drew closer to its source. He felt a wave of nausea grip his stomach.

Lying flat on the ground, Gilly inched his way forward on his belly. The cloud of smoke shifted. He caught sight of a dark figure bent over the fire, swaying rhythmically as though in a trance. The sounds of chanting rose and fell as the man swayed first one way and then the other. Lifting his arms suddenly toward the sky, the chanting figure let out a shrill sound that sent waves of terror the length of Gilly's body. He could see the man clearly now. Blood ran in thin, twisting rivulets down his bare, uplifted arms, and his face was distorted and grotesque with the jagged markings of some bright dye. He wore a necklace of small bones. In his hands he held two gourd rattles that made a hollow, clinking sound with each swaying movement of his arms.

Suddenly the man stopped. Like a statue made of stone, his arms still uplifted, he barely moved a muscle. Gilly's gaze was drawn to the grotesque face, then, to his horror, he realized that the glittering black eyes were staring directly at him. The man moved his right arm slowly downward until the rattle he held was pointed at Gilly.

"Come here, boy!"

It was Cudjo! Gilly knew it for certain before he got close enough to see beyond the jagged streaks of face paint. Shaking with fright, he silently approached the young black man, who remained kneeling before the fire. There on the bloodstained ground beside him lay the torn remains of some poor animal that had fallen victim to the rituals of voodoo sorcery.

Cudjo motioned for Gilly to sit. The boy did so immediately, too fearful not to obey.

"I've been waiting for you," said Cudjo, in a voice ominous with threat.

"Hu—how? How did you know I'd come this way?"

Cudjo's eyes took on a veiled, distant look. His answer came in a low monotone, as though another spoke through him. "Cudjo knows. He has my power. You did not come by choice; it was my power that brought you."

"What . . . what do you want?"

"It's time, boy. Give me the carving."

"The carving? You mean that little figure of the man? I . . . I don't have it. It . . . it's at home . . . in a box."

"No matter." Cudjo's eyes flickered and came to life. "Listen to me." He reached down and picked up a small leather bag lying near the fire. The top was tightly tied with a bit of twine.

"Take this with you. Show it to no one. Tonight, when everyone is asleep, take the carving and this bag and go to the overseer's cabin. Dig a small hole under his front steps and place the bag and the figure into it. Cover the hole well and smooth out the dirt over it. Then go back to your room and say nothing of this to anyone—not even to that worthless slave boy who trails about after you. Do you understand?"

Gilly could hardly speak. He didn't want to touch the awful little bag, much less skulk about in the night with it. Zach's words of warning suddenly came back to him. His friend had been right; he should have thrown that carving as far away as he could when he first had the chance. He could feel Cudjo's eyes riveting into him, as though the young black man were capable of reading his thoughts.

"What . . . what's in the bag?" he asked, trying to stop his voice from shaking.

"It's a conjure bag," answered Cudjo.

"What's a conjure bag?"

"It is not for you to ask questions. Just do as I tell you." Cudjo lifted Gilly's trembling hand, placed the conjure bag firmly into his palm, and then forced his fingers closed around it. Looking into Gilly's eyes once more, he added, "You will do it—tonight!"

Gilly rose to his feet and backed away from the fire. He couldn't take his eyes away from Cudjo's. It was as though they held him locked in a grip. Finally the young black man raised his arm and pointed in the direction of the woodland trail. Gilly turned, stumbled, and then began to run. He could feel hot tears coursing down his cheeks.

Reaching Nutmeg, he threw himself onto the saddle and rode with wild abandon up the steep rise. Kicking the pony's flanks, he drove his poor mount headlong through the thick underbrush. Oblivious to the dangers of the overgrown trail, he rode as though possessed. The sharp vines and jutting branches scratched and tore at horse and rider alike, but still the boy pushed forward. It wasn't until he reached the very edges of the cleared pasture land that he finally pulled the winded animal to a halt.

Looking down into his hand, Gilly saw that the conjure bag was still there. He had to know what was in it! Pulling at the twine with shaking fingers, he finally managed to untie it. Once again the nauseating odor drifted up to him. He shook a bit of the bag's contents onto Nutmeg's saddle. There were small clods of dirt and what looked like dried blood. A broken piece of bone fell out, then a sandy-colored lock of hair. Gilly recognized the hair immediately; it belonged to the overseer.

So that was it—the black magic of a voodoo spell! Appalled by the realization, he felt a wave of revulsion go through him. He was a party to this devilish business! Why had he accepted that filthy little carving—taken it to his own bedroom! What would his mother say if she knew? How could he ever face her again if he did as Cudjo commanded? His mother's words came back to him: "You must never let an evil person have power over your life."

Riding slowly now, he approached the wide lawns of the plantation house. He felt as though his mind were twisting and turning, trying to find a solution to this terrible trouble that had come upon him.

Jeremiah was working in the paddocks beside the stables. He saw the boy approach and, even from a distance, noticed the condition of the tacky. Pushing open the paddock gate, the old groom walked toward the approaching pair, his mouth set in a hard line.

Preoccupied with his worries, Gilly didn't notice Jeremiah until he was almost upon him. When he finally did see the groom, he quickly slid the conjure bag under his shirt. Jeremiah, however, had caught the furtive movement and, studying the boy's face intently, realized that he was deeply troubled.

"Massa Gilly," Jeremiah said slowly as he reached up and lifted the boy from the saddle, "since when you get all dat gumption ta ride dis po' pony half ta death?"

"I . . . I'm sorry, Jeremiah," Gilly stammered. "We were going through the woods . . . something spooked him."

Jeremiah looked directly into Gilly's eyes. "Um-hm. Sho' nuff looks like dis pony ain't de only one what got spooked! Mayhap you best skeedadle back ta de big house an' get cleaned up a might." He wrinkled up his nose and sniffed the air. "Maum Beezie see you, she take you down ta de river an' dunk you in. Dere be a pow'ful funny smell round hey're, an' dat fer true!"

He looked down at the boy's hand still held under his shirt. "You got a bellyache, Massa Gilly?"

Gilly looked down at his stomach with a start but didn't dare pull his hand out. "Uh, er, yeah, that's what I got."

"For sure den, you bes' go see Maum Beezie. Whatever it be what's troublin' you, she fix it."

Gilly nodded and walked quickly toward the house. Maybe that *was* the best solution. Maum Beezie would understand.

Now that he knew there was someone to turn to, he could feel the tears coming again.

Rubbing his eyes with his free hand, he made his way around to the back entrance of the house and tiptoed along the hallway of the servants' quarters until he reached Maum Beezie's door. Keeping his hand well hidden under his shirt, he slid it around to the small of his back, knocked tentatively, waited, and then knocked again.

Maum Beezie opened the door and looked down at the woebegone child who stood trembling in the hallway, his face working hard to fight back the tears that threatened to spill from the corners of his eyes. Placing her hands on her hips, she cocked her head sideways and asked, "Massa Gilly, de world ben hard by you dis day?"

Gilly hiccupped and nodded his head in agreement. "I . . . I got something to show you."

"Den you best come in. Dis hallway ain't de bestest place fer showin' t'ings what gots ta be hid under de shirttails." She pulled Gilly into the room and then turned him around to face her. "Mind you now, chil', Maum Beezie don't want no hoppy toads jumpin' round in she room!"

Gilly nodded soberly, then pulled his hand from behind his back and held up the little bag for her to see.

Despite herself, Maum Beezie let out a gasp. "Massa Gilly! Where from you get dat conju bag?"

"Cudjo. It was Cudjo . . . in the woods . . . by a fire . . . blood running down his arms . . . face all painted . . ." He couldn't finish. Bursting into tears, he fell into Maum Beezie's outstretched arms.

The old nurse held him to her. "Go on, chil', you jes go right ahead an' cry. Sometimes tears be de best medicine." She pulled a hanky from her pocket and wiped his tear-stained face. Setting him on the edge of the bed, her voice came firm and commanding. "Now we gwanna talk 'bout dis, Massa Gilly. We gwanna talk 'bout dis from de beginning ta de end." She pulled her rocking chair close to him and placed her hand gently on his knees. "Best you do de talkin' first. Go ahead, chil'; don't be afraid."

Gradually the story came out, mixed with tears and some prodding questions. Leaning back in her chair, the old woman closed her eyes and began to rock. She was silent for a very long time.

Gilly watched her apprehensively. "Maum Beezie, are you mad at me?"

She opened one eye and squinted down at him. "No, chil', Maum Beezie ain't mad. She love you jes de same as eber."

"Then what are you planning on doing?"

The old woman closed her eyes, laid her head back, and commenced to rock. Finally, after several moments of silence, she opened one eye and squinted down at the trembling child. "Boy, what I be tellin' you is dis: mayhap it aughta be *you* what's doin' de conversin' wid de Lawd. And by-de-by, might wanna tell He how sorry you be fer gettin' mixed up wid all dis fool hoodoo. Now you leave dis conju bag wid Maum Beezie. Come mornin' I spect you gwanna know de answer."

Gilly felt perplexed. He'd felt certain that Maum Beezie would have a solution to his problems; she had been his last hope. Now he could see that she wasn't going to do anything—just sit there and pray. How would that get him out of this mess?

Walking to his room, he thought about her words. She really hadn't ignored him. What she had told him was that *he* had to pray; that's what she meant about "conversin' wid de Lawd." Well, he'd give it a try. It certainly couldn't hurt.

"Now I lay me down to sleep . . ."

All through supper Gilly had tried to think of what to say. He could hear his parents talking quietly in the parlor. Maybe he should just go down and tell Papa. No, that would only make things worse. Papa would have something terrible done to Cudjo, and he certainly didn't want that added to the weight of his conscience.

"I pray the Lord my soul to keep . . ."

It wasn't working. Conversing didn't mean mumbling a rote

prayer. Gilly groaned and sat on the floor. How could he talk to somebody he couldn't even see? How could he be certain that God was even listening? Surely the Almighty had more important things to do than concern Himself with a stupid boy who should have known better than to get mixed up with voodoo in the first place. His mother had warned him. Zach had warned him. Pounding the floor with his fists, he got up and climbed into bed. Perhaps a good night's sleep would help him to see things clearer in the morning.

Later that night he lay in his bed, tossing and turning, unable to sleep. He had repeatedly tried to pray, but the words wouldn't come. Only the mocking image of Cudjo's face, twisted and evil in the flickering shadows on his wall, stared back at him. And then there was the feeling of guilt; that was the worst of all. Maybe it was too late. Maybe the spell was already doing its evil work. If the overseer really did sicken and die it would be he, Gilly, who was responsible.

The night wore into the early-morning hours before dawn, but he could find no rest. It was as though a presence filled his room, pressing on his chest, forcing out beads of sweat on his forehead. Sleep was impossible.

He heard the hall clock strike five, each deep gong seeming louder than the one before. It was no use; he had to do something. Lighting a candle, he tiptoed to his closet, reached up to the shelf, and pulled down the small wooden box. There it lay, illuminated by the candle's small flame—the eyes of the carved face, sightless, as though in death.

Gilly dropped to the floor and began to pray as he had never prayed before, the words flowing out in a torrent of self-accusation. He pleaded for understanding, for help, for courage to do what he now knew must be done. The gray light of dawn was stealing through the slats of the window shutters when he finally arose, dressed quickly, and slipped down the stairs. He made his way along the darkened hallway until he reached the door of Maum Beezie's room. Hesitating only a moment to shift the box to his left hand, he reached up and knocked quietly. There was no answer. He waited and knocked again. This time he could hear a shuffling noise behind the door. He pressed his mouth to the keyhole and whispered her name.

"Maum Beezie? It's me—Gilly. May I come in?"

The door opened slowly, and the elderly woman, still rubbing sleep from her eyes, yawned and smiled down at him. "Come on in, chil'. Reckin dis must be mighty important, you risin' wid de birds." She shuffled over to her rocking chair, sat down, and waited for him to speak.

Gilly held out the box and waited while she examined the carving. "I'm going to see Cudjo, right now, before he goes into the fields. May I have the conjure bag back, Maum Beezie? I'm going to give it back to him, and this carving too. I'm going to tell him that I've decided not to help him with his black magic."

Maum Beezie smiled knowingly. Reaching for the apron she'd hung on the back of her rocking chair, she fished around in the deep pocket and then handed Gilly the conjure bag. "You afraid, chil'?" she asked. "You afraid ta face Cudjo alone? Effin you wants, Maum Beezie go wid you."

Gilly shook his head. "No, I can do it myself." Oddly, he really wasn't afraid. Reaching out, he squeezed the old woman's hand and then turned and headed for the back door.

Night dampness still clung to the tall grasses and dripped from the overhanging branches of the trees as he made his way along the wooded path to the slave quarters. The street was already bustling with activity; the workday came early for the people of the quarters. The plantation bell would ring soon, and they would have to leave for the fields. A large cook pot bubbling over a central fire filled the air with a delicate aroma, but Gilly felt no hunger.

Sleepy children sat on their front stoops while their parents hustled about trying to finish some last-minute chore. He could feel the questioning stares of the adults as he passed, but no one spoke to him. A few doffed their hats respectfully; Gilly ignored them. He held his head straight and his mouth firm and walked with a determined step until he reached

Cudjo's small cabin. Once there, he hesitated only long enough to steady his breathing, then knocked firmly on the rough wooden door.

The door swung open immediately, as though the boy were expected. Cudjo, his face somehow younger and more innocent in the light of early morning, stared out at the white child on his doorstep.

Gilly gave him no time to respond. He thrust the wooden carving and the conjure bag into Cudjo's hands. "Here, they're yours. I don't want anything to do with them. I won't do as you say. I won't be part of your black magic. These things are evil—you're evil!" Gilly could feel his chin begin to tremble, and he fought for control.

Cudjo stepped backward as though he'd been struck. His eyes grew wide with amazement, and then for the flash of a moment, the hard lines of his face seemed to crumble into a look of confused fear. His brazen self-assurance faltered. He tried to form a reply, but the words did not come.

Sensing the conflict going on in Cudjo's mind, Gilly pressed his advantage. "You have no power over me. You don't even have power over yourself. You're weak and helpless. You've sold yourself out to the devil!"

How amazing! Where, Gilly wondered, had he gotten the courage to say such words? He could almost feel sorry for the young black man, who by now was visibly shaken. Had he really frightened him that much? "Cudjo, perhaps it would help if . . ."

He never finished the sentence. Trembling with uncontrolled rage, Cudjo lashed out at him, the flat of his hand missing the child by inches. His battle of the conscience was over. "Don't need your help, white boy!" There was a look of pure hatred in his eyes. "The day is coming—mark my words—the day is coming when you'll wish you'd never known me!"

5

Mary Had a Baby

(1850)

Zach climbed onto the old oak stump and scanned the open yard of the slave quarters. Settling himself Indian fashion, he went through the motions of picking sand fleas from his trouser legs. It was as good a ploy as any, for each time he lifted his head to snap one of the imaginary pests from his fingers, he could glance furtively about and take a few mental notes.

Not much difference, he decided, between this spot and what he'd known back home. The same massive live oaks lined the dirt roadway. Though they bore their evergreen foliage and were festively strung with Spanish moss, they could not alter the disheartening signs of squalor in the houses below. It was a place where dreams died. The dwellings were hovels, with patched roofs and sagging chimneys, their tabby walls crumbling with age and neglect. And though they stood in two straight rows, their forlorn appearance left one with the impression that they were defeated soldiers awaiting death's final blow. The street itself, originating as a well-worn trail at the edge of the cotton fields, first meandered through the woods, hesitated momentarily at the base of an ancient oak, and then straightened its spine just enough to march between the two rows of decrepit buildings. At the end of the quarters, with its mission complete, the road disintegrated, lost in a maze of palmetto scrub and discarded trash.

There were some efforts at decency. Each cabin boasted its own garden plot planted with collard greens, turnips, and a few scraggly vines of field peas. The greenery helped to keep down the dust and hide the sorry sight of the depleted soil beneath. A flock of thin chickens and half a dozen piglets pecked and rooted their way from yard to yard, as oblivious as the children of any division between public and private property.

On the sidelines sat the grandparents, those no longer useful in the fields or sorting sheds. They stationed themselves within earshot of the children but made no effort to punish their lesser infractions. The loss of childhood and discipline in its hardest form would come soon enough. Finally, indifferent to everything but the warmth of the sun, the truly ancient ones slept open-mouthed on their front door stoops. These slaves were to be envied, for their only chore was to await the great emancipator called Death.

"Ya-suh, Lawd," muttered Zach under his breath, "sho nuff looks like home!"

He sat there for a good piece of time, hoping someone would notice him, but the stump only got harder, and an honest-to-goodness sand flea found a hole in his breeches. Scratching his leg with renewed vigor, Zach stifled the urge to call out to the children. Best let them make the first move, he decided.

A shaft of sunlight broke through the leafy canopy above and poked its hot finger against his back. He could feel a trickle of sweat rolling down his spine. It strengthened his resolve not to move. Of course they'd seen him, and though the older ones tried not to let on that they had, the toddlers gave it away. Stopping their play, they glanced at him shyly and then turned to giggle into their hands. All right, thought Zach, if this is a game, I'll wait it out.

The minutes ticked by, and the sun climbed higher. Zach's discomfort turned to concern. Not one of the children was paying him the least bit of mind now; even the toddlers ignored him. Why did these dirty little pickaninnies treat him so coldly? As Zach smoldered with a slow-burning anger, the reality of his outcast status began to sink in. Though living among people of his own race, he was obviously not considered one of them.

The truth was, Zach hadn't lived at Weldon Oaks long enough to understand the pecking order. As a personal servant to the master's family, he *was* different from the rest of the slaves. The house servants were always above the common field hands—that was the order of things. But Zach was even more than a house servant. As companion to the master's son, he stood at the top of the heap. The fact that he had had no choice in the matter made little difference. He was still resented.

The other point that made him suspect was the fact that he couldn't lay claim to any local kin. Even folks like Maum Beezie, advanced in status by dint of talent or fortune, were accepted if they had family in the quarters. Not so with Zach. He lived in limbo, a hemmed-in world suspended somewhere between the black man's slave street and the white man's big house.

Not understanding these unspoken boundaries, Zach clung to the hope that he could gain acceptance simply by making his presence known. "Forget worryin' 'bout bein' pushy," he said under his breath. "I gwanna move in where dey gotta take notice." Moving forward cautiously, he tried his best to act nonchalant. When within a few feet of the group, he began to kick at the clods of dirt that lay along the edge of the cleared yard.

An old man with a corncob pipe stuck in a gap between yellowed teeth opened one eye, yawned, and promptly dropped his head back onto his chest. The other old folks, anxious to catch the last warmth of the waning year and the few moments of leisure left to their faded lives, simply slept on.

Suddenly a cluster of little girls, their voices shrill with excitement, raced past Zach, almost knocking him over in their excitement. The weather was unseasonably warm for this late in December, and the girls were dressed in ragged cotton shirtwaists of a nondescript gray that matched the color of the clapboard shanties that served as outbuildings. Their hair, twisted into numerous little braids sticking out at all angles, bobbed about on top of their heads as they ran.

Close at the girls' heels raced a whooping pack of boys brandishing stick hatchets like so many wild Indians on a scalping expedition. They had smeared their faces with the vermillion juice of some wild berries they'd found in the woods. One or two of them sported the tail feathers of a hapless chicken. The bedraggled feathers stuck out at ragged angles from their dark, kinky hair. Most of them wore little more than short drawers or an old shirt that barely came to the middle of their thighs. The material of their clothing was as gray and threadbare as that of the girls' dresses.

Zach stood aside to let the group pass. He couldn't help but smile and lift his hand to wave at them; they were so much like the children he had known at home. Calling to one of the boys as he passed, Zach momentarily forgot his anger, but he might as well have been one of the lumps of dirt for all the attention he received. It was more than Zach could endure! Picking up a clod, he screwed his eyes shut to keep the angry tears from spilling down his face and threw it as hard as he could after the children.

"Ki! Now don't dat jus' beat all!"

Zach spun around at the sound of the agitated voice. A young woman stood just behind him, her hands planted angrily on her hips and small beads of perspiration standing out like drops of dew on her upper lip. He had no idea where she'd come from, but relief flooded his face when he saw that her anger was directed at the children, not him.

"Dem chilluns hab we plum tuckered out! Effen dey t'ink dat po' ol' Melony's gwanna race 'round behind em all afternoon, dey got another t'ink comin'!"

"Excuse me, mam." Zach touched his fingers to his forehead. He stepped back to let her pass, but she made no effort to move on. Shrugging, he turned away to watch the children, but he could still hear the woman's labored breathing at his ear. The fact that she was heavy with child hadn't escaped his attention.

Just then a string of angry words erupted from the group of boys, who were now pummeling each other in dead earnest. The happy banter had deteriorated into a free-for-all that took on all the earmarks of a violent confrontation. With a surprising burst of speed, the woman sprinted forward and pulled the fist-wielding boys apart.

"Chilluns! Chilluns!" she shouted at the top of her lungs. "How you 'spect ta be ready fer de Christmas Eve celebration effen you don't practice dese songs? Kyan't jes walk up ta de big house an' catawaller like a bunch of banshees! What de massa an' misses gwanna t'ink effen half ob ya'll show up wid bloody noses an' puffed-up eyeballs?"

The children paid little attention to her. She tried shouting over the tumult again, but her efforts were fruitless. Finally, in resignation, she reached down for a small child who pulled at her skirts, lifted him onto her hip, and walked over to the steps of the nearest cabin. Sighing with exhaustion, she sat down heavily and wiped the perspiration from her face with the back of her hand. The toddler clambered onto her lap. She smiled down at him; snuggling him close to her face, she kissed the plump folds of baby fat at the back of his neck.

Zach leaned against a tree and riveted his attention on the woman and child. A pang of something akin to homesickness pulled at the pit of his stomach. There was a strange familiarity to this scene. He tried to pull the memories from the back of his mind. They came slowly, and with them, the homesickness faded. In its place grew a more unpleasant sensation—a feeling of sheer panic.

It was the young woman's pregnancy that brought back the memories. Once again his own mammy was standing before him, her body heavy with child. She was trying to hide her pain and exhaustion, but Zach could still see it in the lines that pulled at the corners of her eyes and in the tight-lipped press of her mouth. Lifting the hoe to her shoulder, she turned her back to him and walked out into the sweltering heat of the cotton fields. In his mind's eye he was a toddler again, no bigger than the child in the young woman's lap. And once again an overwhelming feeling of despair and fear blotted all other thoughts from his mind.

He was standing at the edge of a hot and dusty field watching the cumbersome form of his mammy move slowly along the rows. It was when the merciless sun stood at its highest point in the brassy sky that they carried her to where he waited. There was no time to take her back to the cabin; the baby was already coming. Instead, they laid her under the shade of a red cedar tree to be tended to by a woman whose hands were still filthy from the dirt of the fields. And it was there, like an unwanted whelp, that Zach's brother had been born!

Within three days of the birth, his mammy was back in the fields. She'd handed him the crying infant and walked away, her face set with the same look of hopeless resignation that he now saw in the young woman sitting on the cabin's step.

As the scene was relived in his mind, Zach's anger returned, flaring now into a white-hot fire. There was a foul taste in his mouth and a tight burning sensation in his chest. He wanted to strike out. What right had these people to treat him as though he didn't belong? He was as much a part of their misery as the lowest field hand. So what if they were only children! Wasn't he a child too? Balling up his fists, he spit onto the ground angrily.

"Boy, why fer you lookin' so took wid de misery?"

Zach jumped. The young woman with the toddler was standing beside him again. A tentative smile flickered across her face as she reached out and touched his shoulder. Zach had the strange sensation that she could read his thoughts. He tried to turn away, but her fingers tightened around his collarbone, willing him to look at her. He turned and stared up into her face. It was a plain face, the nose slightly lopsided and the cheeks pinched and thin, but there was a tranquil beauty there that Zach had never seen before. Then, with a flash of insight that only a fellow sufferer can know, he grasped the meaning of the woman's beauty. It came from some deep, personal pain that had been borne with patient acceptance. It gave a character and quality to the youthful face with old, knowing eyes. This woman understood loneliness.

Her voice was almost a whisper as she began to speak. "Pay 'em no mind, boy. Dey jes don' know. De good Lawd, though, He know. Just ask He, dat's all. He take away de pain."

Moving her hand, she laid it softly on his head. To Zach's dismay, the tears started running freely down his cheeks, and the burning sensation in his chest began to fade. He buried his face in his hands and cried with heavy, wrenching sobs.

The woman said nothing for a long time; she simply let him cry. When there was nothing left but gulping hiccups, Zach lifted his head and turned away to scrub at his cheeks with dirty fists.

"Kin you sing, boy?"

"Wh-what?" Zach wasn't sure he had heard right.

"Kin you sing?" she asked again as though nothing else had transpired between them. "We be puttin' together a singin' group fer de Christmas Eve celebration on de lawn ob de big house. Problem is, tryin' ta get dese here chillun's cooperation be 'bout as hard as cornerin' a yard full ob piglets what just seen bruder fox. Effen you kin sing, I'd be mighty obliged ta hab you join in."

"I . . . I don't know. I hain't neber tried."

"Neber tried!" The woman looked incredulous. "All de Gullah folk sing. Matter ob fact, dat's what dey do best. You be Gullah, hain't you?"

"I . . . well, yes-um, I guess dat's what I am. Onliest . . . I don' belong here wid dese folks."

The small smile came back to her face. "Effen you here," she answered emphatically, "you belong!"

Zach felt the tears threatening at the back of his eyes again. He tightened his face to prevent them from spilling out. "Don't look like you makin' much progress wid dis bunch ob chilluns," he said brusquely.

The woman's laughter was like the tinkling of the silver bell that Josephine used to call the planter's family to dinner. "Hain't dat de truth! De harder I try, de worser dey get!"

Zach couldn't help but laugh. "Mayhap I kin help," he said, feeling his self-esteem returning.

"Sure would be obliged effen you could. By de by, dey call me Melony." The woman stuck out her hand, and Zach grabbed at it as though he were being saved from drowning.

"I'm Zach," he said simply. He pointed to the toddler still clinging to Melony's skirts. "Be dat yo chil'?"

A look of pain crossed Melony's face. Zach realized he had said something wrong.

Pulling the toddler close, Melony shook her head. "No, suh, dis boy hain't mine. He mammy be in de fields. I jes look after he during de daytime." She glanced down at her swollen belly, and a strange mixture of hope and despair crossed her face. "Purty soon, dough, I hab my own."

There was another long, uncomfortable silence; then Melony motioned to the door of the cabin. "Effen you rather not sing, dere be plenty other t'ings what need doin'." She waved him on into the cabin.

Zach pushed open the creaky door and walked in cautiously, waiting for his eyes to adjust to the dimly lighted interior. Then he let out a long, low whistle. The entire room was filled with all manner of homemade instruments. There were drums and willow flutes, tambourines and rhythm sticks, gourd rattles and leather straps with bells attached, and in one corner gleamed a store-bought banjo and a shiny fiddle. Zach walked back out onto the stoop and looked at Melony, his eyes wide with wonder.

"Dose be de instruments fer de band," she said, with a twinkle in her eyes. "Now effen you kyan't keep a tune, mayhap you jes as soon be in de band."

Zach was incredulous. Christmas had meant very little at Mount Hope plantation—a single day off with a few extra sacks of cornmeal and, if the master felt especially generous, a bit of coffee and a side of bacon. There had certainly been no reason to celebrate at Mount Hope, Christmas or otherwise. His family had known only years of drudgery and a constant hunger that gnawed at their innards and sapped away even the will to survive. But the thought of an honest-to-goodness celebration appealed to him, and he quickly agreed to lend his support in the practice sessions, though he wanted no part in the actual performance. The fear of further rejection still preyed on his mind.

After much pleading and cajoling on the part of Melony, and with a few well-placed kicks of newfound authority from Zach, the children had finally gotten themselves into some semblance of order. The rhythm band was beating out a cacophony of sound that sent the birds fluttering from their nests and the squirrels scurrying across the ground in frantic search of more distant trees. Spoons clanged against pot lids, dry bones and sticks clattered out an unsyncopated beat, and rattles and drums vied with each other as though in battle, while flutes and whistles of every description added their strident sounds to the general noise. Zach rammed his fingers into his ears and looked at Melony in despair.

Oblivious to the unholy sounds, Melony was moving among the members of the choir, passing out a pile of white robes made of bedsheets discarded from the big house. Held together with an odd assortment of pins and bits of twine, the robes would serve the choir quite nicely for the night of the celebration. Then, within days of the festivity, they would be recycled into more drawers and shirtwaists, which would soon take on the same gray appearance of all the clothing the children wore.

Zach longed to take part in the merriment, but he still felt distanced from the group. Besides, there was something that both fascinated and repulsed him about this idea of providing entertainment for the white family's enjoyment. He could not comprehend how a group of black people held in slavery could possibly want to sing the praises of a white child who had been born centuries ago. They said the infant had been born in a stable among the cattle and oxen, not unlike the shameful birth of Zach's brother; but that didn't change the fact that he was white and therefore, somehow better than other folks. And he was supposed to be a king of some sort, maybe even the son of God. What kind of a king would be born in a stable? What kind of god would let his son be treated so poorly? Well, no mind; that was what folks called "religion," and he had no belief in such nonsense.

By late afternoon, Melony, with Zach's assistance, had the band beating out a few recognizable tunes. Though he might not understand the theological implications of the holiday, this celebrating part of it was proving to be fun. It was with reluctance, therefore, that he turned from the group and went in search of Melony. Unable to make herself heard over the din of the band, she had taken her choir off to quieter pastures for their practice.

"I best be gettin' back ta de big house now, Miss Melony. 'Spect Gilly be finished wid he schoolwork by now, and de missus be wantin' me ta help serve de suppa."

"Scurry along, boy," she said, with a tired smile. "Say how-de-do to my mammy while you at it."

"Yo mammy?" Zach was taken by surprise. "Who be yo mammy?"

"Why chil', don' you know, dat be Maum Beezie."

"Fer true? Oh, yes'm, I like Maum Beezie jes fine. She treat me like I belong."

"Honey lamb, you *do* belong!"

Zach felt like shouting. This Melony, she was just fine. Nodding his head gratefully, he turned away and walked toward the wooded path that led to the big house. But just before he disappeared into the woods, Melony called out to him. "Tell Maum Beezie dat de time soon come."

Zach didn't understand the message but acknowledged that he'd heard it and would let the old nursemaid know. He raced through the woods until he reached the wide lawns. Slowing to skirt the herb garden and kitchen quarters, he made his way around to the back of the house.

Surprisingly, the back doorway was wide open, and a procession of frenzied servants moved in and out, each one laden down with boxes and barrels taken from a nearby storage shed. Josephine stood in the doorway of the cookhouse shouting directions to an equally busy kitchen staff, who scurried in and out with platters of food.

To Zach's delight, not even Josephine had noticed that several of the yard dogs were taking advantage of this easy access to the master's domain. One mongrel came lopping out with a piece of cooked chicken clamped tightly in his jaws. Zach picked up a broom and swiped at the dog, but the wily little creature was under the piazza steps before the broom could even touch him. Shrugging, Zach pushed his way through the line and headed for the front foyer. On his way up the curved staircase, he bumped into none other than Maum Beezie herself.

"Bless my soul, chil'! Where you ben? De young massa been lookin' high an' low fer you."

Zach pulled his head down into his collar. "Ben down in de quarters. Seen yo Melony. She axt we to tell you sumpin'."

"What's dat, boy?"

"She say, 'De time soon come.' "

Maum Beezie's face changed instantly. Lines of concern puckered the skin on the bridge of her nose. Zach waited for a reply, thinking the old woman might enlighten him, but she seemed suddenly preoccupied. Without another word, she scurried down the stairs, leaving Zach with the uncomfortable feeling that trouble was brewing.

He turned and glanced up as the voice of the butler interrupted his thoughts. "Move aside, boy, afore I drop eberythin'." To Zach's dismay, all he could see was legs and feet. The upper half of the pompous butler was hidden by a precariously balanced stack of gaily wrapped packages. The sight struck Zach as humorous, and he broke into raucous laughter. But then, looking up, he found himself staring into the disapproving eyes of Marian Weldon, the plantation mistress.

"Beg yo pardon, mam," Zach blurted, then turned and raced up the stairs.

Marian stopped long enough to watch the young servant disappear into her son's room. It was on the tip of her tongue to call him back and berate him for disappearing when there was so much work to be done, but there was something about this black child that unnerved her. She couldn't quite put her finger on it, though she suspected it had to do with the fact that she'd had no choice in his selection.

Whatever had possessed her husband to bring in a boy they knew nothing about? More than thirty families on the place; surely there was a suitable child among them! Trusting her own people was one thing, but this boy—he was an unknown.

Though Marian rarely voiced her fears, they were always there, waiting to prod at her with icy fingers. A single white family living on an isolated sea island with 160 black slaves; how easy it would be for the mantle of power to change! All they needed was a strong leader, especially one who had learned to hate. Their own people were docile enough, for they'd always been well-treated, but this boy—he had been given a reason to hate. Oh, he might not show it, but it had to be there, festering away in his mind. What would happen, Marian wondered, a few years from now, when he was grown and saw that his position had placed him a few pegs higher than the rest of the people on the place?

Marian shuddered involuntarily. She tried to shake the fear from her mind. This was no time to be worrying about the might-be's of life, but just in case, she made herself a mental note: Zach's presence in this house would be a conditional arrangement. "One misstep," she muttered under her breath, "and I'll see to it that he's out in the fields for the rest of his days!"

Slowly following the butler down the stairs, Marian ruminated over the message she'd overheard Zach deliver to Maum Beezie. "De time soon come," he'd said. As though in response, Marian could feel her own baby moving within her. Her body, cumbersome and heavy with new life, quickly exhausted the little energy she had. She felt restive and agitated. Associating the concern of her own pregnancy with the immediacy of

Melony's message, a chill of fear moved through her. The young black woman had such a history of childbearing problems! Baby after baby now rested in the damp earth by the side of the river, most of them never having known a full day of life outside their mother's womb.

Marian sat heavily on the edge of a chair and watched the butler place the family's gifts under the big evergreen propped in a bucket in the front parlor. She tried to think of the happiness of the coming holiday, but she couldn't get her mind off Melony. Misfortune seemed to trail the woman like a bloodhound. Just five months had passed since William, Melony's husband, had taken Diablo for an exercise run. The horse, difficult for even his master to handle, had returned riderless from the eastern end of the island. It was hours later that they'd brought William's broken body back, his neck fractured and hoof marks on his chest. Melony, once again pregnant, was now left without a husband.

Making up her mind, Marian placed the butler in charge of the decorating and went in search of Maum Beezie. She didn't have far to look. The elderly woman was busying herself in the pantry, stacking the containers of food for the coming holiday in neat rows.

"Maum Beezie?" Marian smiled at the old black woman tenderly.

"Yes'm?"

"I overheard what Zach said to you about Melony. Please, my dear, you really must go to her."

"Oh, no, missus. Eberythin' 'll be jes fine. 'Sides, my place be wid you."

Marian reached out and touched the old woman's cheek. "No, it is not," she said gently but firmly. "Your place is with your daughter right now. It will be hard for her without William. Besides, my time is still a few days off. Run along back to the quarters. I'll manage quite nicely here on my own. Gilly won't be any trouble. Do you know, I hardly see hide or hair of him since he's gotten Zach."

Maum Beezie clucked her tongue and looked troubled. She

had no great confidence in the servants. "Hain't right I should leave you, missus. Dese house niggras spend more time palaverin' den dey do workin'!" Nevertheless, she looked infinitely relieved when she scurried out of the house minutes later.

By sunset on Christmas Eve the activity on the plantation had subsided to a happy buzz. Marian managed to label the last of the packages for the people of the quarters and had the butler set them out in orderly stacks along the front piazza. The house servants, dressed in their finest, pulled rocking chairs close to the wide top step and then stood behind as the family filed out and seated themselves.

Gilly, with Zach standing at his side, trembled with anticipation. His own presents awaited him under the big fir tree. The candles fastened to its outstretched branches would not be lighted until the yard ceremony was over. Fearful of the possibility of fire while they were otherwise occupied, Papa insisted that the lighting of the tree should be saved as the grand finale of the evening.

A hush fell over the grounds as darkness descended. Then from the distant stretches of the woods came the sound of singing. Sweet and high, the lovely music drifted through the evening mist—the happy sound of children's voices. Closer and closer they came. Soon little twinkles of light, like the fireflies of summer, flickered through the trees. Mothlike, the children glided from the dark woods, carrying with them the dancing flames of candles. Their voices rose to the rhythmic sounds of the beautiful Christmas spiritual:

> Mary had a baby, ay Lord.
> Mary had a baby, ay my Lord.
> Mary had a baby, ay-a Lord.
> De people keep-a-comin,
> But de train done gone.
>
> Where did she born Him, ay Lord?
> Where did she born Him, ay my Lord?

Where did she born Him, ay-a Lord?
De people keep-a-comin,
But de train done gone.

Now the women added their voices to those of the children.
The group moved toward the piazza, swaying in unison as
they walked:

Born Him in a manger, ay Lord.
Born Him in a manger, ay my Lord.
Born Him in a manger, ay-a Lord.
The people keep-a-comin,
But de train done gone.

The men stepped forward and joined the choir, their deep
voices giving body and resonance to the song:

What did she name Him, ay Lord.
What did she name Him, ay my Lord.
What did she name Him, ay-a Lord.
De people keep-a-comin,
But de train done gone.

In a grand chorus, they lifted their faces to the dark sky
and sang the final verse. The house servants moved down the
steps to join them. Even the planter's family stood up and
added their own voices to the rhythmic beauty of the song:

Named Him King Jesus, ay Lord.
Lily of de Valley, ay my Lord.
Prince of Peace, ay-a Lord.
De people keep-a-comin,
But de train done gone.[1]

All was hushed. For just a few moments the people of the
big house and the slaves of the quarters were as one. Zach
stood quietly behind his young master. He had been deeply

touched by the words of the song. Who was this King Jesus, anyhow? Why should slaves sing about Him with such reverence? Perhaps Melony would explain it to him. His eyes searched the silent crowd gathered on the lawn, but he could see nothing of the young woman.

It was hours after the people had returned to the quarters that Maum Beezie came walking slowly back to the big house. Awakened by what sounded like wailing coming from the direction of the quarters, Zach slipped out of bed and went to his window. The thin light of a waning moon made dark shadows in the yard. One of them was moving. He pressed his face against the window and recognized the bent form of the old woman. She was carrying a small bundle in her arms and moved as though she were in pain.

Tiptoeing to the top of the stairs, Zach listened to the hushed whispers in the hallway below. The mistress was waiting for Maum Beezie in the foyer. She opened the door wide and pulled the elderly woman into her arms. He could hear them sobbing together. Suddenly Zach knew why he had not seen Melony with the people of the quarters at the Christmas Eve celebration. The old fears that had tormented his mind when his mother lay in the pangs of childbirth returned. With a terrible certainty he knew the truth—added to the line of small graves in the moist earth by the side of the river lay the body of his new friend, Melony!

His heart breaking, Zach staggered back to his small bed. Pounding his fists into the pillow, he gave free reign to the last shreds of pent-up frustration. Would there never be an end to his pain? He had wanted to ask Melony about this Jesus of whom the choir had sung, but now she was gone. What good had all of her religion done? How would it help her baby, left motherless? The joy that he'd found was gone, and in its place the anger returned.

Below, in the dimly lighted parlor, Maum Beezie and her mistress struggled with the same conflicting emotions. For them, however, the terrors of childbirth fever were only the beginning.

"Shall I find a woman to take the child for you?" asked Marian, her heart aching for the grieving grandmother.

Maum Beezie shook her head. "De good Lawd put dis chil' in my hands," she said, with rising determination. "I reckon He give me de strength ta do whatsomeber be needed ta care fer she."

Marian pushed back the blanket and looked at the tiny black face. "Oh, she's so pretty! What will you call her?"

"I is gwanna call her Angel," said Maum Beezie, " 'cause dat's jes what she be," and she smiled tenderly through her glistening tears as she looked down at the infant.

"May I hold her?"

"Sho nuff."

Marian reached for the babe and was surprised at her feathery lightness. She reached under the blanket and touched the perfect little fingers. Thrilled by the feel of them, she slid her hand down the silky smooth body—to the scrawny but well-formed legs—until she came to the tiny feet. There, she stopped, and a look of anxiety touched her face.

Maum Beezie's jaw tightened as she watched her mistress. Her hands went out as though to prevent the inevitable discovery of flawed workmanship in this child, whose mother had been swallowed by the hungry, but never satisfied, mouth of the grave. How could she bear one more pain added to so many others that weighed upon her shoulders and threatened to strip away her last bit of faith in a caring God?

Marian sensed the woman's agony and hesitated. She lifted her eyes to Maum Beezie's and saw the jagged shadows of pain within them. With a nod of resignation, the elderly woman reached out and took the infant back into her arms. Then, as though the act would forever bind her to this new girl-child she held, she moved her trembling hand down and pulled away the blanket to expose the tiny feet. An involuntary gasp passed the mistress's lips.

Maum Beezie bowed her head and touched her lips to the child's forehead. "Don't neber no mind," she said quietly. "Don't neber no mind at all. Twisted feet ain't gwanna stop dis baby from being loved! She me little angel." The baby cried from the draft of cold air touching her tiny body. "Hush-a-by, chil'. Don't neber no mind. Even twisted feet is gwanna walk in heaven."

Marian cupped her hands over the two tiny clubfeet and let the tears flow freely.

6

Conjure Doctor

(1851)

Spring came quickly to the Low Country and touched the Sea Islands with its gentle magic. Soft rains and zephyrlike breezes drifted across the landscape, turning the marsh grasses into a swaying verdant carpet. Myriads of sea creatures, large and small, entered the watery web through the wide, tidal estuaries to spawn in the protective bays and quiet stream beds. Before their perilous return to the sea, the survivors and eventually their young would feed upon the rich detritus caught between the thick grasses and oozing mud banks. With the coming of spring, the Low Country savannahs were transformed into a productive nursery that knew no equal.

If, however, the coming of new life was both magical and perilous for the creatures that swarmed through the wet savannahs, so, too, it was for their human counterparts who lived upon the dry land above the sand dunes. And nowhere was this more apparent than in the slave quarters. The infant of a slave was only of value if he or she had the potential for physical labor. The malformed were looked upon as worthless, and, therefore, dispensable. No one understood this better than Maum Beezie. Hadn't she brought more babies into this world than she cared to remember?

That terrible night when Melony lay dead, with her crippled

newborn still desperately sucking at her breast, the practical aspects of what needed to be done had weighed heavily on the old woman's mind. Every midwife knew that for a deformed and orphaned slave child, death was more easily achieved and surely more merciful than life. The temptation to snuff out the tiny spark that separated the living child from its dead mother was almost more than she could bear. With shaking and hesitant hands, she lifted the squalling baby from Melony's cold breast. The tiny mouth quivered as it was plucked away, as though pleading for survival; and with that, Maum Beezie's resolve crumbled like the ashes of burned paper.

Lifting the infant toward her own warm breast, she pressed it close and crooned a wordless tune that was both a mournful dirge and a haunting lullaby. This tiny bit of life was all she had left of her own sweet daughter. How could she destroy it? No, it was impossible! With her owner's consent, and God willing that she live but a few years more, she would raise the child herself. The old woman had been a slave too many years to make the weighty judgment on her own, though. Tucking the infant into her shift and wrapping herself in a warm cloak, she set out for the big house. The final decision belonged to the plantation mistress as surely as did this newborn child. If the mistress rejected the baby, then Maum Beezie's only recourse would be to plead that the two of them be sold off together, though who would be fool enough to buy them she could not imagine.

There was, however, no need for worry. Marian Weldon had too gentle a heart to be practical in the hard business of bartering with human lives. When, on that fateful night, the two of them met at the open doorway of the big house, Maum Beezie had only to look into the mistress's eyes to know that all would be well. Even when the revelation of the child's deformed feet was made, the agony of the moment was softened by her mistress's look of sympathy. They had hugged each other, wept together, and for that small moment of time, the differences of skin color and social status evaporated. From that day on, the crippled child, known as Angel, became an integral part of the master's household. It was a position, considering the poor circumstances of her birth, for which she would later be grateful.

A new year dawned, and once again the miracle of birth was carried out, only this time under considerably more fortunate conditions. Laura May Weldon entered the world on a blustery, cold day, the tenth of January, in the year 1851. The warm confines of her parents' soft feather bed were a far cry from the rope-slung bunk and the drafty walls of a slave cabin. Her mother's hands, though used to work, had not been roughened with calluses from the repeated friction of a hoe handle. There were white muslin sheets for her to lie upon and soft flannel gowns trimmed with delicate lace and satin ribbons to cover her tiny, perfectly formed body.

Master Weldon was jubilant! He'd had a bumper crop of cotton last season, and now to cap off his good fortune he had a newborn daughter. Life seemed to be reaching that point of perfection, he was certain, his own rigid sense of discipline and careful husbandry had brought him. Unable to discern the future, with its two-edged sword of war and the boll weevil that would bring the South to its knees for several decades, Gilbert Weldon also failed to recognize the deadly scourge already beginning to eat away the lifeblood of both his family and his homeland—human slavery.

Gilbert, after all, was a good master. He was benevolent to his house servants, seeing them as an extension, though several pegs lower, of his own family. He accepted the presence of Maum Beezie's granddaughter in his home as the natural order of things. When the child came of age, the old woman would find useful work for her. In the meantime, although Angel's feet were useless, his wife would be glad for some extra hands. And so with that thought classified and filed away, he promptly dismissed the black child from his mind, for the intricacies of running a household were of no major concern to him.

The master's field hands were another matter. They, like the oxen in his barns and the cattle in his fields, were there to carry out the work of the plantation. If they failed to perform that function, they had no place on his land. To that end, the hands were kept fit and well-fed. The care of their young was equally important, for each healthy child would one day mean another healthy field hand. Even the elderly, those few who survived to be so labeled, must be allotted their share of food, shelter, and a resting place in the sun.

Gilbert saw this as an extremely equitable system. In fact, he often considered his people worthy of envy. Owning nothing, not even their own lives, they had no need to worry over the heavy responsibilities that he himself carried as a constant burden. Their homes, their food, their clothing, and their work were all provided. The fact that they had no choice in the nature of any of these commodities never entered his mind.

There were, of course, a small handful who stood out from the general crowd. These few were respected by the master because they had special skills that gave them a position of some standing. Jeremiah the groom and Gullah Jim, the old Negro fisherman who had in his youth been both mentor and friend, stood high in Gilbert's estimation. And more recently he had taken notice of a new buck who seemed perfectly suited to serve as his right arm in the vital business of maintaining discipline.

Cudjo had caught the master's attention some months ago, and despite the strenuous objections of the overseer, had been given a steadily increasing amount of authority over his fellow slaves. He was obviously intelligent and possessed a natural air of leadership. Good slave drivers were hard to come by, but Cudjo seemed a perfect fit for the task. He cared not a fig if he was unliked—or even hated. He spoke distinctly, and his voice carried well, even over the work chants and the loud digging sounds of the hoes. He sensed how to pace the hands to get a maximum day's work from them, yet his haughty attitude kept them in awe of his authority. And though Master Weldon would never sanction the use of a lash as punishment, Cudjo had become adept at using its sharp, cracking sound as an impetus for keeping the laggards at their work.

Sitting in his study on the night of Laura May's birth, the master of Weldon Oaks found great contentment in reviewing the record books for the past year. He made it a practice to be meticulous in his accounts, and he also liked to keep a concise journal of those things he deemed important to the running of his plantation. As he flipped through the pages of the account book for the past year, he stopped occasionally to read some of his short entries. One in particular caught his eye:

> *June 2, 1850.* Extended dry spell. Corn beginning to shrivel. Sold yellow cotton in Beaufort for 6 cts/bale. Purchased new female, Phoebe, aged 17 years—$550. Potentially good breeder. Replaced broken plow blade. Set women to thinning cotton and men to collecting sedge for compost.

Phoebe! Yes, he should have thought of this before. It was high time he mated Cudjo, and perhaps Phoebe would do. He rubbed his chin contemplatively and tried to fix a picture of the young Negro woman in his mind. The last time he had seen her she'd been on the way to the wash house with a basket of clothing balanced on her head. Her lithe grace and erect posture had made him suck in his breath. She had wide hips, a good sign for childbirth, and her skin was the color of dark honey. Her face was finely molded; high, prominent cheekbones and a small, pointed chin carried proudly over a long, slender neck. Her almond-shaped eyes gleamed with intelligence and good breeding. A mulatto, most likely; he'd been lucky to get her for such a low price.

Gilbert stood up and walked to the darkened window. Clasping his hands behind his back, he turned, paced toward his desk, then returned once more to the window. Yes, they would be the perfect match. Besides, he needed to upgrade his stock.

Walking back to his desk, he began leafing through the pages of his record book once more. Another entry made him stop short.

> *October 25, 1850.* Sent Samuel down to Dr. Judd's for
> medicines. Outbreak of dysentery. Lost 3 children—
> 2 males and 1 female. Samuel very trustworthy.
> Shows strong interest in Phoebe. Will consider
> mating.

How had he forgotten that? Samuel was a likeable-enough
buck, and he had the strength of two men. Gilbert drummed
his fingers on the desktop, trying to come to a decision. No,
Cudjo was a far better match for the high-born Phoebe. What
a pair they'd make! Dismissing Samuel from his mind, the
plantation master reached for his ledger for the new year and
turned to the second page. With his pen he wrote:

> *January 10, 1851.* Daughter, Laura May, born this day.
> Healthy and well-formed. Marian, thank God, has
> no complications and is resting well. Decision made
> to mate Cudjo to Phoebe. 2 hogs killed for bacon. 6
> bales of white cotton ginned and packed.

Blotting the ink off his latest entry, Gilbert yawned and
closed the book with a satisfied thump. He'd send for Cudjo in
the morning and make arrangements for the wedding within
the month. Marian, of course, would probably not be out of bed
before the end of the week, and he always preferred to have
her notify the woman of his decisions in these matters. No
problem with that. It wouldn't hurt to have Cudjo know of the
arrangements a bit ahead of time. It would give him the opportunity to court the girl.

Cudjo, it turned out, was more than satisfied with the
arrangements. He'd had his eye on Phoebe for some time,
though she made a practice of passing him by as though he
were little more than a pane of glass. Her studied indifference
had rankled him plenty, that and the obvious fact that she
was sweet on a no-count field hand named Samuel. Despite
his hatred for the master, Cudjo had to admit that the man
was doing him a good turn in this matter. Samuel would prob-

ably bellow like a mad bull when he found out, but there was little enough he could do to alter the decision—for the master's word was law.

Deciding to press his advantage, Cudjo let word leak out about the impending match to several of the younger bucks who looked to him as a man of leadership. He was hardly prepared, however, for the vehemence of Samuel's reaction. The man actually had the gall to come at him with a pitchfork, which Cudjo barely managed to fend off. Had it not been for the lash hanging loosely at his side, which at the last moment he managed to coil around the upraised weapon, Samuel would have impaled him then and there.

Cudjo did not hesitate to report the incident to the overseer, being careful to leave out the obvious motive for the assault, and arrangements for punishment were hastily made. Samuel was placed in chains and locked in a narrow tin shed designed especially for the most dangerous offenders. There he stayed for ten days, shivering in the cold of night and sweating through the day, when the sun lay heavy on the metal roof and not a breath of air moved. For two days he had neither food nor water. On the third day, and each day thereafter, he was given only one cup of lukewarm water and a few crusts of bread.

It was a dire punishment, but Cudjo was not satisfied. How his fingers itched to lay his lash hard across Samuel's bare hide! When the dog was finally let out of his pen, the threat of a second attack would be as certain as the sunrise. When it came, Cudjo had no doubt that Samuel would have the upper hand, for Cudjo would be no match for that brute's size and strength. Yes, if he were to tip the scales in his favor, he'd have to do it now. Cudjo instinctively knew that a cunning mind was, in this case, the best self-defense.

But as he had ruminated over the past few weeks, Cudjo began to get a sour taste in his mouth. Perhaps things weren't going as well as he'd thought. Was this situation with Samuel unnerving him, or had he made some wrong decisions along the way that were now interfering in his ability to think quickly? His worst mistake to date was that he had been fool enough to play lightly with the fears and emotions of the master's son. That episode with the conjure bag had been foolhardy. And to make things worse, in the heat of anger he'd gone as far as nearly striking the boy! Thankfully, that obnoxious little buckra knew how to keep his tongue in check, or it would be he, Cudjo, and not Samuel, who was spending his days in the tin shed! He would have to be more careful in the future, but if nothing else, Cudjo was willing to admit his mistakes and learn from them.

The first step, of course, was to practice the fine art of keeping oneself under firm control at all times. To do that, Cudjo knew he'd have to, for the time being, let someone else perform the sacred rites of the snake god and the magical spells of voodoo. The inducement of a trance left him too vulnerable to error, and he was not, as yet, well-versed enough in the intricacies of black magic to carry them out independently.

Then there was that miserable little nigger boy, Zach. *There* was a fly in the ointment that he hadn't counted on! Thinking to buy the brat's loyalty with bribes, he had carved small figures and offered them as special favors. The ruse hadn't worked; though still a child, the boy was too wise in the ways of the slave quarters to be so easily fooled. Abandoning kindness, Cudjo had settled on the use of threats, but even the element of fear seemed to have little effect on the boy. Cudjo now realized that Zach was a force that must eventually be reckoned with in a firm and final manner.

Sitting at the doorstep of his cabin, Cudjo watched the moon crest the loblolly pines and disappear behind a band of fast-moving clouds. There would be rain tonight; he could smell it in the air. With the temperature steadily dropping, it would probably turn to ice by morning. No matter, that would suit his purpose well, for the slaves in the quarters were certain to stay huddled close to the heat of their fires. Nor did he have to worry about the people in the big house, for they were still celebrating the birth of the master's new daughter and would hardly be concerned about the whereabouts of a common driver.

Cudjo's one fear was the possibility of running into a patrol. If he was caught skulking about on Ladies Island in the middle of the night without a pass, things would not go well for him. He'd have to avoid the roadway as much as possible, though he strongly disliked the thought of trying to find his way through the maze of deep woods and wet marshlands that cut through the island with no predictable pattern. His best bet was to go by way of the river.

Sniffing the air like a lion on the hunt, Cudjo pushed himself upright, secured his small pack between his shoulder blades, and slipped unnoticed into the dark line of trees behind his cabin. How he hated the buckra, that insufferable pack of jackals which forced upon him the need for stealth!

It was well past midnight by the time he found himself polling up the fast-moving Morgan River toward Ladies Island. He'd managed to secret away an old flatbed boat several weeks ago. His abilities as a boatman were negligible, but he'd had enough common sense to pay attention to the changing of the tides. Now it was only a matter of riding in with the current and finishing his task in sufficient time to catch the outgoing tide back to Coosaw. Finding the old man's shanty would be the hardest part of the trip.

Cudjo, it turned out, was lucky. Just as his informant had said, the river narrowed slightly as it turned southward into Lucy Point Creek, and there ahead, protected by several small hammocks, lay the little inlet that led into the marsh. He made a mental note of each turn, trying to fix on some landmarks that would aid him on the outgoing trip. Here was a half-dead cypress tree leaning into the creek, and there a mud flat bristling with a bed of sharp-edged oyster shells.

As he rounded the last small hammock, the eerie call of a hunting osprey broke through the stillness of the night. Pushing his pole hard into the bottom mud, Cudjo slowed the boat, cupped his hands over his mouth, and returned the call. There was no reply. He waited in breathless silence as the seconds ticked by. Perhaps he'd been mistaken. Perhaps it had been a real osprey after all. Letting his craft drift with the current, he scanned the sandy embankment with its high crest of thickly jumbled scrub. Nothing moved. Only the first cold drops of rain rustled against the foliage and made small plunking sounds in the brackish water of the marsh.

Then he saw it—the glint of highly polished metal on the uppermost part of the embankment. Lifting his hands to his mouth once more, he mimicked the call of the osprey. The answering challenge came from the direction of the shining metal disk.

Only after Cudjo had stepped out onto the sandbar did he see the man. He appeared to be very short—or was he simply bent over with age? His kinky hair lay matted against his head, and there was a bluish sheen to his face. The bronze disk that he wore about his neck was as wide as the moon at its quarter, and now Cudjo noticed that he also wore thin bands of bronze about his upper arms and around his ankles as well. The skin on his face and chest was pockmarked with a series of tattoos, though their forms could not be discerned in the dim light.

Reaching out his hand, the man touched Cudjo's face with his long, talonlike fingernails. "De marks ob Poro be on you," he said simply, then turned and disappeared into the underbrush.

Cudjo hesitated, not knowing if he should remain where he was or follow. Hearing nothing, he pushed his way through the thick growth and suddenly found himself standing in a small clearing. The old man was now squatting behind a small fire, poking about through the burning embers with a long stick as though searching for something. Behind him rose the dark shape of a log hut barely tall enough to accommodate even the short man. A mongrel dog poked its head out of the entranceway and then retreated to growl menacingly from the dark interior.

The old man hissed a warning at the dog and then motioned for Cudjo to sit. "Straight from Africa, hain't you, boy?"

Cudjo resented the use of the word *boy* but contained his

irritation. "Been a few years now," he said, "but I haven't forgotten." He chose not to elaborate on exactly what had not been forgotten, deciding that the old man, if he truly knew his business, would not need to ask.

After a long silence, the old man lifted his eyes to study Cudjo in the firelight. "Talk right nice fer a niggra, don' you, boy? Sound jes like de buckra."

Cudjo simply nodded.

"Don' want no part ob de ol' ways, I reckon," said the man.

Cudjo surprised himself with the strength of his response. "That's not true, old man! The ways of my ancestors are important, but the shores of Africa are far across the great sea. The voices of our gods are lost in its depths."

The conjure doctor looked knowingly at Cudjo. "Dem ol' gods—dat who you come here ta find?" he asked quietly.

Cudjo nodded.

Without another word, the man reached out his hand and grasped an earthen bowl that lay near the fire. Then, evidently having found what he'd been searching for amongst the embers, he lifted from them some odd-shaped bits of burned wood and threw them into the bowl.

Cudjo waited patiently for the incantations to be finished. The words sounded both strange and familiar to him, since he'd heard them before in the distant past of his childhood. The rains began in earnest, but the conjure doctor ignored them. Water began to stream in ragged rivulets through his matted hair and across his shriveled shoulders and chest. Cudjo could feel the cold seeping into his very bones. He tried not to look at the old man, who was still hard at work with the soggy mixture lying at the bottom of his bowl. With a final hiss, the small fire flared momentarily and then disappeared. Cudjo glanced back at the darkened river, worrying that the conjurer was moving too slowly.

"The tide's changing, old man," he said with frustration.

"Kyan't stop de tide."

Cudjo gritted his teeth. "I have an enemy among the slaves. Is your medicine powerful? Can you place a curse on him?"

The old man grunted and continued to work at the mixture in his bowl.

"I'll pay you well."

"What you got ta pay wid, boy?" The conjurer's words were harsh and mocking.

"With silver coins."

At that, the old man snorted with glee. "Silber coins! What I do wid silber coins; buy me freedom mayhap?"

"Perhaps," answered Cudjo in measured tones. The old man was taunting him. He had a strong desire to reach out and grasp his scrawny neck—to snap off his head the way one would snap off a chicken's.

"With chickens," said the conjure doctor.

Cudjo jumped. Had the old fool read his mind? No, that's what he wanted in payment—chickens. Well, that would be easy enough. Cudjo felt relief, for he would have had to steal the coins from the master's house, a chore he hardly relished. Trying to smile, he nodded at the voodoo worker. "It's as good as done. When will you work the curse?"

"Been done," echoed the old man. Then dismissing Cudjo with a wave of his hand, he stood up, scratched at his buttocks, and hobbled through the door of his log hut.

"Wait!" shouted Cudjo. "I haven't told you the name of my enemy."

The cackle of insane laughter came from the dark mouth of the hut, but try as he might, Cudjo could get no further response. Finally he turned away and walked back to the boat. The tide had already started to ebb, and it took some effort to lift the boat from the sticky mud and push it far enough out to set it afloat.

The first light of dawn was touching the eastern horizon when Cudjo slipped back through the shadowed woods toward the slave quarters. He could hear the mournful sounds of wailing. Now what? Had another one of their dirty little brats died? They'd been dropping like flies of late, what with the chilly rains of winter and the foul-smelling mud that seeped into everything.

Slinking around the corner of his own cabin, Cudjo noticed a small knot of people gathered about the door of the dwelling where the single women lived. The plantation bell was clanging insistently in the background, calling the hands to the cotton fields despite the drizzly, cold rain. He'd have to pull himself together and get this motley bunch going, or the overseer would have his hide.

Picking up his lash, he walked purposefully toward the group of people standing in mournful silence near the woman's house. "Mayhap yo'll ain't bright enough ta hear dat bell!" Cudjo lapsed into a form of Gullah, using it only when he wanted to mock the ignorant savages he was forced to live with.

No one spoke to him or even turned their heads his way. There was a shuffling sound coming from the cabin and then another long, sorrow-filled moan. Cudjo looked up just in time to see Samuel step through the open doorway. In his arms he carried a limp figure tightly wrapped in a blanket. The women around him began to chant a wordless, durgelike tune used for the dead.

A cold shockwave worked its way up Cudjo's spine. He stumbled backward, almost afraid to ask the question. "Who—who is it?" he stammered.

One of the younger women turned her accusing eyes on him and then spit the answer into his face. "You had aughta know, driber man!" Reaching out, she lifted the blanket to reveal the lifeless face and sightless eyes of Phoebe.

7

Mo' Love Somewhere

Samuel ran the tip of his finger along the outstretched wings of the graceful wooden swallow at the top of the new grave marker. What artistry! And it was so fitting for a woman who loved the beauty of nature. If only he could have carved it himself.

His hand dropped to his side. He now realized that he despised himself as much as the craftsman who had created this exquisite carving. Worse than that, the jealousy he felt toward the man threatened to destroy the one thing that could pull him through this terrible time—his faith.

Sinking to his knees in the mud that covered the new grave, Samuel let his head drop into his hands while he wept. He had tried—goodness knows he had tried to show her how much he loved her. And Phoebe had loved him in return, he was certain of that.

Someone touched his shoulder softly. Turning his face upward, Samuel looked into the sorrowful eyes of Jeremiah. The old man said nothing but simply nodded, squeezed Samuel's shoulder, and then walked away. Was that pity he had seen in the man's eyes? Pity for what? The loss of Phoebe, or Samuel's inability to stand up to Cudjo?

It had been a shameful scene there at the grave. Of course, the old man felt his disgrace. Jeremiah knew him so well and supposedly had been grooming him to one day step into his shoes as spiritual leader of the community. To Samuel's tormented mind, Jeremiah's silence was a mute testimony to the disgrace that he now felt.

He was alone; one by one, the other mourners had drifted away. A cold drizzle was falling, turning the already-sodden earth into a quagmire, but Samuel could not leave. There was too much to think about.

"Phoebe, honey, you know dat I loved you."

Silence. Only the whispered sounds of rain dropped gently on dry leaves.

"Phoebe, I tried. Honest I . . ." What was he doing, sitting here in the mud talking about love? He was a fool; no wonder the people pitied him! What good was love when your body and mind belonged to another? He was a slave. He and Phoebe were nothing more than cattle—to be bred at the whim of their master.

Pounding the ground with his fists, Samuel cried out in agony. The sounds echoed off the river, mocking even his despair for something that could never have been. Despite his ardent desire, Phoebe was not meant to be his. Cudjo—rot his black hide—had told him of the master's arrangements.

Gritting his teeth with the burning memory of his shame, Samuel's hate welled up within him. Lifting his eyes, he stared toward the river. There, just barely visible in the heavy mist that crept and clawed along with ghostly shadows, was all that remained of the grave marker he had labored so hard to make. Its splintered end pointed at him like an accusing finger, mocking his inept stupidity. Again Samuel could see Cudjo's smirk of disdain as he looked at the grotesque carving and ripped it out of the ground. Then he snapped it in two and replaced it with his own beautiful workmanship.

"It's *my* marker that belongs here," Cudjo had said with finality. "She would have been mine. You know that the master promised her to me."

How could Master Weldon have even considered giving Phoebe to Cudjo—Cudjo, that wiley adder who conversed with the devil! The thought was too repulsive to contemplate. No, never! Far better if the master had taken her for himself.

Samuel turned from the grave and walked slowly away. Misery and the mist covered him like a shroud. In the distance he could hear singing. He concluded that his people were still in mourning, though it was unusual for them to hold on to their grief for so long.

But then, as Samuel drew closer to the quarters, the words of the song became more distinct. Perhaps he was mistaken:

> I never been t' heaben but I been tol'—
> I look back an' wondah how I got ovah.
> The streets up dere are pave' wid gold.
> I look back an' wondah how I got ovah.
>
> If you get dere afore I do—
> I look back an' wondah how I got ovah.
> Tell all my friends I'm comin' too!
> I look back an' wondah how I got ovah.

Just then Jeremiah stepped from the shadows and stretched out his hand. He pulled Samuel toward him and laid his arm across the young man's sagging shoulders. "Ben out in de wilderness facin' de tempter, habn't you, boy?" he said quietly.

Samuel's eyelids flickered. He could say nothing.

Jeremiah leaned over and grabbed the broken handle of a hoe that had been left propped against a nearby tree. "See dis he'e hoe?" he asked.

Samuel looked down and nodded.

"De handle on dis hoe was made ob weak wood. Come toil an' trouble—pop, pop—he snap in two."

"Sumpin' like de bad wood ob my grave marker?" commented Samuel, bitterness lacing his voice.

"Now, boy, don't confuse we. Hain't de same t'ing—hain't de same t'ing, no how. We discussin' de tool, not de workman."

Samuel grinned in spite of himself and waited for the old

man to continue.

Turning the hoe over in his hands, Jeremiah pointed to the blade. "De blade, howsomeber, dat be anuder matter. Made ob strong metal, tempered in de fire, honed sharp by de wheel. Come toil an' trouble, blade don' snap. Get rusty from de rain, mayhap, but wid a bit ob scrapin' an' scrubbin', purty soon he shine like-anew." Looking up through his bushy eyebrows, Jeremiah added for emphasis, "An' dat fo' true!" Then after a short silence, "Hear me talkin', son?"

"Yes, suh, bruddah Jeremiah, I hears you talkin'."

"You made ob metal like dis hoe blade, Samuel. De Lawd put you true de fire an' hone you on de wheel. Den He look down an' say, 'Mm-mm, me-oh-my, dat be a fine man I gots me! T'ink I use dis man to spread de Word.' "

Now Jeremiah's voice dropped to a dramatic whisper. "Purty soon, 'long come de debil. See de Lawd's fine-lookin' man. Chuckle to heself an' slap he knee. Say, 'Lessee, mayhap we kin mess he up a mite.' Den he spit in yo eye, drop rain on yo head, turn you rusty like dis hoe blade."

Samuel was dumfounded. Could it be? Were Satan and the Lord really contending over an unimportant person such as himself?

Warming to the subject now, Jeremiah's voice trembled with enthusiasm. "Now de La-w-d, He see what dat m-e-a-n ol' debil be doin'. Look down 'pon brudder Samuel. Say, 'Satan, dis man hain't fo' you. Dis Me man. Take yo foot in yo mouth, debil, 'for I heist you up an' chuck you out.' An' dat ol' Satan, he slink off into de bushes.

"Den Gawd look at you, Samuel, shake He head, an' say, 'Hol' still, boy, 'cause I 's gwanna hab ta do some mighty hard scrapin' an' scrubbin'.' "

Samuel felt tears stinging the back of his eyes. "Dat fo' true?" he asked in a small voice.

"Um-hmm, dat fo' true. Purty soon you shine like-a de mornin' sun 'cause you ben made ob good metal."

Samuel's face was wreathed in a smile now. Pumping the old groom's hand up and down, he said, "Jeremiah, someday

I's gwanna be a preacher man jes like you."

Jeremiah shook his head knowingly. "Yes, suh, dat's what de Lawd be waitin' fo', bruddah Samuel. Dat's what all He scrapin' an' scrubbin' be 'bout."

The singing began again, and Samuel's heart seemed to swell with the words. Lifting his head proudly, his deep, bass tones joined the voices of the others. Strange, he thought to himself as he sang, that trip to the side of the river had turned out to be more like a baptism than a funeral. The moving words of the spiritual drifted up through the trees like a prayer:

> Dere's a bright side somewhere.
> Dere's a bright side somewhere.
> I'm gwanna keep on 'til I find it.
> Dere's a bright side somewhere.
>
> Dere is mo' love somewhere.
> Dere is mo' love somewhere.
> I'm gwanna keep on til' I find it.
> Dere is mo' love somewhere.

Some slaves, however, had not discovered a release for their misery. They carried enslavement as if they had been placed in a harness with an immovable oak. Cudjo was such a man.

Phoebe's sudden passing had, at first, been a mystery to Cudjo, as indeed it was to the others. How could anyone understand the death of an apparently healthy person? But while most of the Gullah folk simply chose not to question the ways of providence, Cudjo found it easier to blame the event on the evil spirits—the hags and plat-eyes that came with the fog which clung to the rivers and deepened the darkness of night. The old ways, the old gods, were still an intricate part of Cudjo's makeup. Christianity, he decided, was only for the weak who had given in to the will of their masters.

Coming directly from Africa's shores, Cudjo had no doubt

that his departed ancestors were displeased with him. He believed them to be a part of the great pantheon of deities that served as the messengers for a supreme but entirely remote God; as such, it was their role to dispense earthly judgment. Despite his bravado, his fear of the spirits' anger held him in the greatest bondage. The thought that his bungling attempt to call upon the powers of voodoo had destroyed the one person whom he eventually might come to love nearly undid him. But in the end his love for self was stronger, and he found ways to rationalize the tug of his conscience.

Now his hatred for the white planters grew with the intensity of a forest fire. It was *they* who had enslaved him; *they* who killed Phoebe; *they* who took away the old ways and the knowledge of the ancient gods. Worse yet, he felt that many of his fellows had given in like a herd of dumb cattle. Were they no longer men? Were not their fathers once warriors? Did they not have the strength and pride to face their masters—to rise up and destroy them? It was then that the vision of his ultimate mission came to him. He, Cudjo, had been appointed by the ancestral spirits to lead his people from the bonds of slavery. It was a marvelous revelation! Determining that he must now channel all of his efforts to the great task, his first objective must surely be to so ingratiate himself with the master and his family that when the time for armed rebellion did come, the shock of surprise would assure total victory.

Creeping into his cabin, Cudjo slept fitfully that night. The sounds of prayer and singing annoyed him. He tried to block out the words, but they kept resurfacing in his brain. Morning could not come soon enough as far as he was concerned.

8

De Prayin' Grounds

(1853)

The first pale rays of a late October sun pushed aside the mist that hung along the horizon. They filtered through the soft curtains of Gilly's bedroom window and touched the striped wallpaper above his headboard. A mockingbird was happily singing from the top of the china-berry tree just outside his window. Gilly listened to the little minstrel with his eyes closed. When the song was finished, he lifted one eyelid and looked toward the source of the narrow stream of light. Had there been a frost last night? He prayed that there would be.

Sliding his bare feet from beneath the warm feather comforter, he felt for the floorboards with his toes. *Brr!* It *was* cold. A frigid draft of air worked its way up his legs. He wrapped the comforter tightly around his body and tiptoed to the window, moving like a cat on ice. Pushing aside the curtains and pressing his nose against the pane, he noticed that his breath formed small, misty clouds that obscured his vision—a good sign, he knew. A quick wipe with the comforter gave him a clear view of the river winding its way through tidal marsh flats and exposed oyster beds. Cord grass rippled in the stiff breeze and lay drying in drifted piles along the bases of the sea walls.

Gilly's bedroom window in the Beaufort house faced east, a happy circumstance as far as he was concerned. Sunrise over the river and its bordering marshes was his favorite time of day. The marsh grasses were turning from green to soft yellow-brown, but the early rays of sunlight gilded their edges with gold. Opening the window just enough to let in a brisk draft of air laced with the light autumn smell of the marshes, he shivered and pulled the comforter closer to his chin.

Coosaw, he knew, lay just beyond that wide stretch of land called Ladies Island. How he wanted to be back there! The hot summer months had seemed so boring; he had thought they would never end. Unlike his parents, Gilly did not find the family's yearly sojourn in town to be a pleasant break from routine. He longed for the wide savannahs and deep woodlands surrounding their island home.

Forced by the dread threat of malaria to desert the outer islands during the hottest time of the year, planters like Gilly's parents set up housekeeping in their spacious, white-columned mansions along the Beaufort waterfront. There, surrounded by the luxuries that only a prosperous town could afford, they were able, for a few months, at least, to forget the grinding workload of their larger land holdings.

But at age eleven, Gilly still had enough of the child in him to prefer adventurous play above all else. This enforced gentility was more than he could endure; he found himself looking for ways to be mischievous. On this fine September morning the opportunity did not take long in presenting itself.

He moved his gaze down through the branches of the chinaberry tree until it reached the shaded lawn below and let out a whoop. There *had* been a frost! Its lacy white coat still clung to the shadowed grass and transformed the yard into a fairyland! He could scarcely contain his excitement.

At this point the aroma of breakfast drifted up from the window just below his. Leaning over the sill he called out at the top of his lungs, "Hey, Jo, wat ya' cookin'?"

A few seconds passed before the wooly head of Josephine the cook popped out of the lower floor window. "Massa Gilly, you best stop dat screechin' lak-a-de jay bird!"

"Wasn't a jay bird, Jo. It was a mockingbird!"

"Don' neber mind wha' kinda ob bird he be. I done tol' you

onest iffen I hab tol' you a hondad time, dis hey'r ain't no way to axe we fo' breafist! Jes when you gwanna git cibilize, boy?"

Snickering under his breath, Gilly reached over to a nearby branch, pulled off a handful of the sticky yellow berries that still clung to the chinaberry tree, and showered them down on Josephine's head. "Look out, Jo! It's starting to rain. Best pull your head back in and get to cookin' some chittluns for breakfast."

"I'm gwanna gib you deese hey'r chineeberry fo' breafist, iffen you keep a deblin' we lak-a-dat!" shouted back Josephine with indignation. "Hen's eggs be what I's cookin'—an' hen's eggs be wha' you's eatin'! You jes keep unrablin' dat mouth outen da winda, boy, and yo papa gwanna be 'roun' hey'r wid de stick!" And with that final warning, the red bandanna disappeared through the window frame.

"Hominy!" shouted Gilly as loudly as he could. "Don't forget my hominy."

Suddenly, the door to Gilly's room was flung open. There, sure enough, stood Papa, his hands planted firmly on his hips and a look of anger pulling his mouth into a hard line.

Wow, Papa was really mad!

"It's six o'clock in the morning, and prior to your outburst your little sister *was* sleeping quite soundly. Gilly, you know perfectly well that that poor child has been ill. Your mama's been up half the night with her." Papa walked across to the open window and slammed it shut, then scowled down at his son. "Young man, has it ever crossed your mind that other people in this house might enjoy a little peace and quiet once in a while?"

"I'm sorry, Papa. I won't do it again."

"See to it that you don't!" Papa turned and started to leave, then thought better of it. Spinning around again to face his son, he added, "And instead of spending the day looking for trouble, suppose you clean up the mess in this room and get yourself packed. We're going back to Coosaw tomorrow."

Gilly waited until he could no longer hear his father's footsteps in the hallway, then made a flying leap across the room, pushed up the window, and thrust out his head. "Wooppee!" he shouted. "Josephine, did you hear that? We're going back to Coosaw!"

The trip was made in a large bateau with the family's trunks and boxes packed in an orderly square at its center so as to balance the load. Mama and Papa sat in rocking chairs placed just to the front of their luggage. Papa talked of the coming season and how he would rebuild the sorting and carding sheds. He also wanted to dig a new well just to the south of the poultry shed.

Mama, on the other hand, had it in her mind to reactivate the Cotillion Club. While living on the plantation, she had virtually no contact with women of her own race. The islands' social club afforded at least an occasional opportunity to renew friendships. She would not, however, take too much time from her duties as mistress. The people of the quarters needed blankets and warm clothing. In one of her boxes there were three large bolts of wool; she would set the plantation seamstresses to work as soon as she arrived.

Two-year-old Laura May, her eyes wide with the wonder of this new world of light-dappled water and tree-shaded shoreline, sat on her father's lap and chattered happily to the latest cornhusk doll made for her by Maum Beezie. Despite an entire family of perfectly lovely china dolls that had come by steamer all the way down from Boston, Laura May still loved her cornhusk doll the best. The doll's name was Martha, and even when her body began to unravel and her seed eyes fell out, she could always be put together again to look as good as new. As a matter of fact, there had been a whole succession of Marthas, each loved as equally as the one before.

Gilly, on the other hand, was at the prow, his bare feet dangling over the side of the boat into the coffee-colored water below. Zach sat beside him, a cane fishing pole held loosely in his hands. He really didn't care if he caught a fish; it was just so nice to be sitting in the sun and watching the riverbanks glide past. Zach loved to hear the Negro boatmen sing with their deep, resonant voices:

> Roll, Jordan, roll, Jordan,
> Roll, Jordan, roll.
> Little chilluns, learn ta fear de Lawd,
> An' let yo days be long;
> Roll, Jordan, roll, Jordan,
> Roll, Jordan, roll!

They kept perfect time with the sweep of their long oars. Maum Beezie, sitting in another rocking chair to the back of the piled-up boxes, hummed along with the boatmen's song as she watched little Angel, who was playing on the deck near her feet.

The little black child, though nearing the end of her second year, could still not walk. She crawled about on her hands and knees, sometimes pulling herself upright so that she stood on the outer edges of her deformed feet. It was obviously a strain for her, and she seldom stayed that way for long. Maum Beezie looked at her granddaughter speculatively. Perhaps Jeremiah could fix up a pair of crutches for the child. She must make a note to talk to him about it when he brought the carriage horses out to the island at the end of the week.

The house servants were lined up and waiting for them on the dock when they arrived. To the master's surprise, there stood the slave driver, Cudjo, dressed in a clean white shirt and sporting a broad smile.

"Mornin', massa," said Cudjo, touching his forehead in greeting. "Sho is good ta habe de fambly back!" With a quick movement, he jumped forward and caught the line thrown out by the lead boatman. Then, nodding and lowering his eyes respectfully, he reached out his hand and helped the mistress deboard.

Only Maum Beezie seemed to have caught the young slave driver's sudden shift in speech patterns. As he reached for her valise, she pulled her mouth sideways and spoke in a low voice so only he could hear. "Now don't dat beat all! Sound like de peacock been out nestin' wid de crows."

Cudjo stared at Maum Beezie's back as she hobbled up the rise toward the big house carrying Angel in her arms. "There'll come a day, old woman," he said through clenched teeth, "when you'll wish you'd treated Cudjo with a little more respect."

The family settled into the old routine quickly, for there was much to be done. The season's first sweet potatoes were ready for digging; this crop would be the staple food for the slaves through most of the winter. But there had also been a good growth of open cotton in the southwest field, and because cotton was where Master Weldon made his money, the decision of which chore should be done first was never in question.

Going down to the fields to meet with his overseer, Mr. Weldon called him aside to lay out his plans for the next few days. "Ned, I want all hands out in that blown cotton; I feel for certain that we've got a bumper crop there. If you can just get these people working a little faster, I'm willing to bet that each one of em' could bring in a good forty pounds per day."

"Yes, sir, Mr. Weldon, but they gotta have enough time for spreading. That always slows 'em up some."

Both Gilbert and his overseer knew that picking cotton was no easy chore. Every handful required care, first removing the cotton from the bolls and then separating out the leaves and small bits of pod. When a picker finally filled the long bag he carried over his shoulder, he had to dump the load on a spread sheet and separate it out so it would dry in the sunshine. While spreading the cotton did slow the picking process, it also gave each hand a break from the more strenuous and tedious task of picking.

Ned, the overseer, was tough, but basically a good man. He knew better than to overwork his field hands, and in his own way he could usually restrain the master from coming up with unrealistic expectations for them. This season, however, he hadn't counted on having to deal with an overly ambitious slave driver.

It wasn't just luck that sent Cudjo walking to that edge of

the field as his superiors were making their plans. Throwing caution to the wind, he moved closer, took off his hat, and cleared his throat to get their attention. "Beggin' yo pardon, massa," he said in what sounded to him like a humble tone, "couldn't help hearin' ya'll talkin' 'bout dis hey're cotton crop."

The overseer was flabbergasted. How dare this brazen young buck, slave driver or not, presume to talk directly to the master? But to his surprise, Mr. Weldon turned to the young black as though interested in what he might have to say.

Cudjo was encouraged to press on. "Appears to me, suh, dat dis whole pickin' business might jes move along right smart iffen de pickers didn' stop ta do any spreadin'. I been told dat, on some plantations, dey hab one or two people ta collect de cotton. Den dey jes haul it all up to a separatin' shed fer dryin'."

The overseer snorted in disgust. "We don't do it that way here, boy! The master likes his cotton dried in the sun. Now get back into that field—and see to it that those pickers keep up a steady pace."

Cudjo shuffled back toward the rows of cotton. Master Weldon stood and watched him speculatively for a while, and then to the consternation of his overseer, called him back. "Cudjo, come back here for a moment."

"Yes, suh, massa."

"Well, Cudjo, I like a driver who can think." He turned to the overseer and placed his hand on his shoulder. "Now don't get your nose pushed out of shape, Ned, but I think Cudjo's got a good point here. Just because we've always done something one way doesn't mean we can't try it another way for a change."

"Yes, sir, of course that's true. But you've always said that sun drying is best. Besides, a full day of nothing but picking 'll be pretty hard on the hands, sir."

"Won't last but a few days," interjected Cudjo. "Den you kin gib 'em off half a day ta rest up."

Gilbert clapped his young slave driver on the back. "Now

that's a right fine idea. I must say, Cudjo, you're a good man to have on hand!"

Cudjo smiled to himself as he turned and walked back into the fields. The elevation in title from "boy" to "man" had, in itself, been worth the risk he'd taken. Why, in a few more months he'd have these fools eating right out of his hand!

No one complained over those next hard days of steady picking, but in the evening, when the sun went down behind the loblolly pines, the field hands had all they could do to prepare their meals and care for their families. Still, if they knew it was Cudjo the slave driver who had suggested this cruel pace, they said nothing about it.

As for Cudjo, he decided to simply lie low for the time being. After the final day of picking, when he heard the mutter of drums in the night, he simply closed himself in his cabin and ignored the furtive whispers that moved through the quarters like cats on the prowl.

The half-day off was a welcome relief for everyone, as they had gotten far behind in their personal chores. But when night came the drums began again, and this time they were more insistent. Something was afoot, and the excitement of the people could hardly be contained.

Gilly lay in his bed listening to the distant sounds of the drums. Even he could tell that there was a difference in their quality. Finally, when he could take the suspense no longer, he snuck out of his room and went to seek out Zach.

Zach could not sleep either. He, too, had heard the drums, and though he was not privy to their meaning, he knew there was danger in the messages they sent.

"Listen, Zach," whispered Gilly conspiratorially, "something important is going on, and I aim to find out what it is."

Zach's eyes grew wide with fright. "Oh, no, massa Gilly! You mus' neber go out dere lookin' fer dem drums. Bad t'ings goin' on dat de slabes don' want de buckra ta know 'bout."

"If they don't want the whites to know about it, then they shouldn't be beating the drums so loudly; they'll have the patrol after them for certain."

Zach was alarmed. Perhaps he had said too much. The fact was, he *had* heard some talk of a meeting tonight, though where it was to be held he had no idea.

Gilly was already pulling on his clothes. "Are you gonna come with me or not?"

"Please, massa Gilly, don' make me go!"

"All right, then, if you're afraid of your own shadow . . ."

Gilly had returned to his room and was putting on his shoes when Zach walked in, a sheepish look on his face. "I hain't lettin' you go out dere by yo'self. Iffen you fixin' ta get yo neck wrung, best I come wid you."

The boys went down the trellis just outside of Gilly's window. Had the drums stopped? No, a sudden shift in the wind brought their sound back again. "Over there," said Gilly, "to the northwest." They started out with a loping trot and had barely entered the woods when they heard the sounds of many stealthy footsteps.

"Get down," whispered Zach frantically.

They fell to the ground and crawled on their bellies until they could see through a small clearing in the heavy scrub undercover. Through the dark shadows outlined only by starlight, many black feet were moving. They walked stealthily but surely toward the sound of the drums.

Suddenly Zach's memories of home were jogged, and he let out a gasp. "De prayin' grounds!" he said under his breath. "Dey is goin' ta de prayin' grounds."

Gilly turned to face his young slave. "Praying grounds? What does that mean?"

"Don' know what it means," answered Zach, "but dat sho nuf be where dey's goin'. Look-a-dere, Gilly." He pointed to a wider area on the path. Many dark shapes were moving along it. "See fo' yo'sef. Hain't jes de menfolk. Dere be womuns an' chilluns too."

They waited there, hugging the ground with their bodies, until they were sure that the last person had passed. Then they pushed themselves upright and followed behind at a careful distance.

Gilly had no idea how far they'd gone, though he was certain that they were far into the deepest woods on the island. He had never been here before, and if it weren't for Zach by his side, he might well have lost his courage and gone back by now.

The drums had stopped, but somewhere up ahead he could hear what sounded like the clapping of many hands. Zach tugged at his sleeve. "Best we slow up now an' get back down on we bellies," he said in a whisper.

The flickering of firelight was ahead of them, and Gilly remembered a recurring dream that he'd had when he was younger. It was a vision of Indians dancing through the fire— and a fierce old man dressed in a coat of white feathers.

The ground underneath felt cold and damp, but they could hear the distinctive sound of voices, and they forged slowly ahead. One voice carried above the others, and there was something strangely familiar about it.

Finally they could go no farther without being seen. Ahead of them, in a large clearing lighted by a roaring bonfire, stood a circle of slaves. Their bodies swayed from side to side in unison, and occasionally one would lift his hands toward the darkened sky and shout in a loud voice, "Hal-le-lu-jah, bruddah, tell de story!" Then the others would respond, "Yes, Lawd. Yes, suh, Lawd. Ju-bi-la-tion day comin'!"

So that's what this was, thought Gilly. A religious service. And all this time he had thought they were plotting a slave rebellion. Still, there was something fascinating about what was going on out here. He turned to look at Zach and was surprised at the expression on his young slave's face. The black boy was staring ahead in rapt fascination. Gilly's eyes followed the direction of Zach's stare. There to the left of the fire stood a figure wrapped in a long white robe.

Gilly's heart beat harder, and he felt his fingers tighten into fists. Was his dream coming true? Had the fierce old Indian brave come back to Coosaw after all?

The figure lifted his arms and swung them wide, and then

he turned in their direction. Gilly gasped. It was Jeremiah! What was he doing here? Did Maum Beezie know?

Gilly pondered these questions as he hugged the damp ground, his eyes wide with wonder at the animated movements of the man in the white robe. It was as though some of the leaping flames, having found their way into Jeremiah's body, were now surging through his eyes and mouth.

Gilly knew that Papa himself had chosen the old groom to be the spiritual leader of the plantation's slave community; it was a common-enough practice. Within each plantation community, one man, usually someone advanced in years and well-respected by his fellow slaves for his deep religious convictions, was chosen by the master to "bring Christianity" to the benighted members of his race. These men were given the title of Praise House Watchmen, and though the private congregating of more than a very few people was strictly forbidden by law, they were encouraged to speak often about the values of Christianity. Of course, there could be no talk of Moses leading the children of Israel from slavery. Jeremiah had always been carefully instructed in the subject matter that he was to present. The apostle Paul's admonition to slaves was one of the more frequent topics chosen: "Urge bond-slaves to be subject to their own masters in everything, to be well pleasing, not argumentative, not pilfering, but showing all good faith that they may adorn the doctrine of God our Savior in every respect" (Titus 2:9, 10, NASB).

To keep the gatherings as small as possible, Papa had built a tiny chapel just big enough for the watchman and perhaps four other people. Appropriately, it was called a "praise house," and most plantations on the Sea Islands had one. The services, like those conducted by the itinerant ministers, were to be held in a subdued and reverent atmosphere. And because the slaves were also strictly forbidden to learn reading and writing, the need for a Bible was eliminated. The watchman was taught by the visiting pastors, or perhaps by the master himself, to memorize those texts appropriate for presentation. It had seemed like a very equitable system to Gilly when he'd first heard about it.

But what he now saw was such a vast change from the orderly religion of the plantation that he could hardly believe his eyes. The deferential posturing and halting speech patterns were gone. Jeremiah, living up to his name, spoke with the power of an Old Testament prophet. His voice rose and fell, reverberating from the shadows as he told the biblical stories of sin and forgiveness, bondage and deliverance. "You he'r me talkin', chilluns?" he called out to his congregation.

"Amen! Ya-suh, bruddah!" came the unified response. "Hal-le-lu-jah! Tell de story!"

Now his listeners were warming to the subject, and there was nothing one-sided about the service. It grew with power and emotion as the tide grows with the full moon. "*You* be de chilluns ob Israel!" shouted the preacher. "De day ob jub-la-tion comin'—comin' soon! Sing ha-le-lu-jah, chillun'!"

Even the trees seemed to shout back, "*Hal-le-lu-jah!*"

"Yo bruddah, yo sistah, need deliberance from bondage. He'r we talkin', chilluns?"

"Ya-suh, Jeremiah. We he'r you talkin'."

"Yo bruddah, yo sisteh, gwanna trabel dat dark highway ta freedom—gwanna follow de drinkin' gourd in de sky."

Jeremiah's voice hesitated, then rose in a new crescendo. "What you gwanna do, chilluns? What you gwanna do while dey trabel dat highway?"

"Gwanna pray, Jeremiah! Gwanna pray to de Lawd fo' deliberance!"

Then, as the stars twinkled down on the assembled company, the circle of bodies began to move. Their shouts carried them into the rhythmical chant of a spiritual; its beat welled up within them, moving their glistening bodies back and forth in swaying unison. They kept the beat with their hands; then their feet took up the rhythm—a long line of black bodies moving and swaying in a side-stepping shuffle. The beat grew stronger, and the bare feet slapped against the packed earth, the legs never crossing and never hesitating. The words came loud and strong:

Ah do dearly lobe ta tell,
Ben down in-to de sea;
Christ ma Lawd does all t'ings well,
Ben down in-to de sea.
Hal-le-lu-jah, Hal-le-lu-jah,
Hal-le-lu-jah, Lawd.
Ah ben down in-to de sea.

The "shout" went on into the last hours of the night, with Gilly and Zack transfixed by what they were witnessing. Those who tired of the movement stepped to the sidelines to recover their strength, but they kept the beat with their hands. The entire ceremony was like a piece of Christianity gone African. It was this, and not the hoodoo and voodoo of the conjurers, which truly kept alive the old cultural heritage from one generation to the next.

The night was wearing on, and despite the commotion, Gilly found himself fighting sleep. He pressed close to Zach and whispered a question into his ear, "How long can they keep this up?"

"Till mornin', mos' likely."

"What! But, Zach, if they don't get back in time to go into the fields, Papa will . . ."

"Dey be back in time, Massa Gilly. Dey be back." Then pointing to his own head he whispered, "Gullah folk be plenty sma't. Dey set 'emselbes out a watchman ta keep he eye on de sky ta de east. Den, when de mornin' star come ober de horizon, he gwanna shout out de signal."

Wanting to see if his young master comprehended, Zach shifted his weight onto one elbow and studied the white boy's face. "An' iffen you blink yo eye onest too many," he added, "might be you t'ink dat all dem folks hab jest heist 'emselbes up an'—poof—fly away!"

Gilly felt a shock of surprise. Having seen most of these people as nothing more than subservient field hands, Zach's revelation left him with more questions than answers. Perhaps the planters *were* right. Perhaps the slaves *were* plotting revolt. But surely this ceremony had nothing to do with insurrection! It was a religious service, primitive, and more pagan than Christian. No, Gilly decided he must watch closely and think more carefully about what he was seeing.

Rubbing his tired eyes, he tried to force himself to concentrate, but the steady beat of the music was becoming hypnotic, lulling him into lethargy. Try as he might, he could no longer focus on the group of slaves moving about in the clearing. Finally, cradling his head in his arms, he closed his eyes and drifted into a fitful sleep. In his dreams he saw again a band of Indians dancing before a roaring fire. This time, however, the medicine man dressed in a robe of white egret feathers was a black man—none other than Jeremiah, the plantation groom. The incantations that he sang were oddly familiar, filled with the words of a Gullah spiritual.

Gilly was awakened suddenly by a sharp cry coming from somewhere nearby.

"Mornin' star risin'! Mornin' star risin'!"

Zach had been right! With a speed that left Gilly speechless, the company dispersed and melted into the woods as though they had never been there. Only the circle of packed earth left in the clearing told of the clandestine meeting. The slaves returned to their bondage, but with their minds and spirits strengthened by a new sense of identity and purpose.

Of course, Gilly knew that this meeting in the woods was entirely illegal, and he should report it to Papa immediately. He had a strong feeling that there was some deeper meaning to Jeremiah's words about traveling the dark highway to freedom and following the drinking gourd in the sky. But then he remembered the look of pure joy on those black faces and the exuberance of the people as they moved in unison to the music of their own singing, and he knew in his heart that he could never disclose their secret. It was enough for now to know the source of the drums.

9

The Fugitives

(1855)

The two fugitives huddled close to the sandy embankment, ignoring the cold nibble of the waves that were being pushed higher by the incoming tide. The man was worried. He pulled his young wife closer, sheltering her from the bite of the cold November wind that swept across the river from the north. Had he found the right spot? Would the bateau reach them in time? Would its elderly skipper even be able to see them before they had been discovered by the dogs?

Even now he could hear the deep-throated baying of the hounds as they strained at their leashes. He knew what to listen for. When the barking of the dogs became shrill, their capture would be certain. The light rain gave the animals difficulty in keeping the scent, that and the fact that he and his wife had sloshed through enough marsh and swamp to last them a lifetime.

"Nell, honey, you sure dat you ain't too cold?" It was a silly question; he realized it immediately. Of course, she was cold! He was too. Their clothes were in tatters from the flight through the grasping vines and thickets. They were caked with mud, and their feet and legs were cut and bleeding from the sharp marsh grasses and oyster beds. If only she weren't pregnant!

Nell being with child was something they had not counted

on when they planned this flight for freedom. But they had no choice; he was sure of that. They were going to be sold off to help pay the mounting debts of an ill-managed plantation on St. Helena's Island. Their master had repeatedly assured them he would sell them together, but who could tell what a new master might do? Then again, their present owner could hardly be taken at his word, for he had often reneged on promises as well as debts. Few of his fellow planters trusted him, and he was both feared and hated by his slaves.

Ben often wondered why the whims of fortune had so seldom tilted his direction. When he and Nell had first gotten wind of the news that their master was about to sell them, they set about making plans to gain at least a shred of control over their destiny. There was, however, little that they could do. Knowing that some planters treated their slaves better than others, they quickly decided that their best chance lay in a local sale. Weldon Oaks stood at the top of the list as far as "good plantations" went. The trick, of course, was to humbly approach the master and suggest that he make inquiries.

But Ben had never gotten the opportunity to talk to his master; the man had had more important things on his mind than the discomfort of common field hands. Deciding that his next move should be to contact one of the Negroes of Weldon Oaks, Ben made inquiries. Gullah Jim, that was his man. The old slave from Coosaw was known far and wide for his fishing skills, as well as his freedom to travel unchecked throughout the islands and waterways of the Low Country. The summons, however, had to be sent out with great care, for lives were always in the balance when the slaves of one plantation communicated secretly with those of another. Reverting to their ancient African ways, they used the drums. During the darkness of night, when the white master had settled himself into the comfortable confines of his "big house," the coded messages would travel for miles across the flat, marshy landscape, racing from island to island with the speed of sound.

When the call came, Jim was both compassionate and anxious to help, but things never seemed to work out the easy way. Having an unquestionable "in" with Massa Weldon, Jim didn't hesitate to drop a few well-placed hints. When those failed, he came right out and asked. The master, however, knew better than to get himself burned by a planter whom he considered nothing but a wily old reprobate. He knew the man well enough to see that he cared nothing for either the lands bequeathed to him or the humans under his control. Any slaves coming from such a poorly managed place would be too hard to handle and not worth the effort to retrain.

Thus, with all of their options for a local sale exhausted, the dangerous plan of escape became more appealing to the young couple. Ben, however, would never have worked up the courage to pull it off on his own. He had been too cowed by years of abuse, and now he had Nell's safety to consider as well. It was only after Jim told him about the secret highways and clandestine organization of the underground railroad that the young buck finally mustered enough gumption to make his move. Surprisingly, it had taken no great effort to convince Nell that it was their best hope.

Ben thought back now to that time of decision and wondered if he had been a presumptuous fool. Scanning the eastern horizon, he could feel his apprehension growing with each passing second. The river was churning toward them now, its waves growing choppy with a building storm. If Jim didn't find them soon, they'd drown like cotton rats caught on inundated mud flats.

Then suddenly he glimpsed the silhouette of a dark form moving swiftly along the crest of the waves. It was the small bateau, its sprit sail billowing out in the heavy wind. Ben knew that he had to signal the skipper, for he might easily miss them in the darkness. Throwing caution to the wind, he stood erect and let out a shout.

His signal was answered with an echoing call, but not from the river. The patrol was coming hard up Sam's Point Road. Ben could hear the shouting of the men and the shrill keening of their dogs. The animals had their scent, but it was his shout that had revealed their hiding place. How close were they? He just had to look. Scrambling up the embankment, he reached its crest and immediately flattened himself to the earth.

The dancing flicker of torchlight could be seen coming down through the trees, the flames twisting grotesquely as the wind from the river buffeted them. At this distance the men looked like frightening apparitions. The capes of their oilskin slickers blowing out in the wind gave them twice the breadth and half again the height of normal men.

In the end, however, it was the torchlight that was the salvation of the two slaves. Indeed, the patrol had spotted them, but the tongues of the flame also served as a signal to the man in the bateau. His boat sailed straight and true for the embankment, disappearing momentarily from sight as it was swallowed by the trough of a wave. Fearing capture more than a watery grave, the two fugitives made a desperate dive into the icy waters, trying to reach the little boat before the heavy seas capsized it or drove it onto the beach. A strong hand grasped them and pulled them over the gunwales just as the first baying hound hit the water's edge.

Only an expert could have turned that little bateau into the wind and guided it back to the wide expanses of the river, and Jim was exactly that kind of boatman. It was none too soon. Rifle fire shot passed them in the darkness as their craft dipped behind another wave. But the patrol couldn't gain a good sighting in the moonless night; their shots fell wide of their mark.

For a long time Ben lay huddled in the bottom of the vessel, trying to gain the strength to sit upright and thank this man who had come like the angel Gabriel to deliver them. When he finally managed to pull his head over the gunwale, his eyes were drawn back to where they'd been. There, fading into insignificance on the fast-receding shoreline of Ladies Island, were the little pinpricks of light from the patrol's torches. In Ben's mind he could hear the angry curses and violent threats that even now must surely be ripping through the shroud of darkness.

"Jim." Ben's voice quavered from cold and fright. "Mah Nell

an' me, we hardly knows how ta thank you. Tain't nothin' we got ta gib 'cept de words. Howsomeber, I been thinkin' mighty hard on dis. Bes' you come wid us, Jim. Dat patrol, dey done seen dis boat, an' sure as you born, dey know who owns she!"

Jim scratched his grizzled beard and sniffed at the wind. "Dark night, dark Nigra. One Nigra look same as anuda in de dark." He chuckled under his breath. "Dis li'l ol' boat, she move so fast—look like de heabenly chariot what pluck up 'Lija. No suh, dem buckra tain't gwanna know de dif'rence."

At any other time Ben would have enjoyed Jim's humor, but he felt Nell shudder, and he reached down to encircle her with his arms. Pulling her close, he tried to use his own body to shelter her from the stinging salt spray driven by the icy wind.

Seeing Ben's concern, Jim reached behind his seat, pulled out an old sailcloth, and gently used his free hand to wrap it about the woman. He had to keep his other hand firmly on the tiller, for they were now nearing the mouth of St. Helena's Sound, and the breakers were coming at them with a fierce vengeance.

Jim knew he had to calm his passengers, so he decided to make some small talk. "Mighty neighborly ob dat patrol ta shine out dem to'ches like-a-dat," he said, trying to make his voice sound nonchalant. "Ol' Jim, he be near ta Brickyard Point by dis hey're time widouten dem to'ches."

The young couple made no response. They huddled quietly in the bow, the trauma of the night heavy on their faces. Jim decided to let them be. Besides being soaked to the skin, they must surely be exhausted. What with the violent rolling of the boat and the biting wind—it was a bad night for taking their leave, that was certain! He had to give them credit, though. Even a seasoned seaman would have found such conditions hard to handle.

To make matters worse, the close call on that riverbank was only the beginning of the trials awaiting this young couple. The next one was even now hard upon them, although Jim had no intention of alerting them to that fact. Locating the waiting steamer in this storm would be tricky seamanship, of which not even Jim felt confident. If, indeed, the good Lord *was* with them, He would have to provide nothing short of a miracle.

It wasn't that Jim lacked faith. In fact, he had a good measure of it, or he never would have agreed to such a precarious plan. And thanks to Jeremiah he had gained a fair insight into what kind of perseverance this bid for freedom would really require. The groom had explained it to him on that night when they sat together at the praying grounds waiting for the shout to begin.

"Dey gwanna hab ta make it all de way ta dis place called Canadie," said Jeremiah. "Must be a mighty far piece, 'cause dey gotta chase dat north star till she be nearly oberhead." The tone of his voice had hushed to a whisper then, as though even the southern constellations might reveal their secret.

"Why so far?" asked Jim.

"Be sumpin' called de Fugitive Slabe Law," answered Jeremiah, "a bad law, an' dat fer true! Go ta Philadely, dat law'll get you. Go ta Boston, get you dere too. Put you in chains an' carry you back ta de massa. Den, dear Lawd, betta you neber been born!"

"Canadie," said Jim, his voice distant with thought. Then, after some reflection, "Dat law kyan't catch you in Canadie?" The truth was, Jim was having second thoughts about placing this couple in such a hazardous position. Perhaps they'd be better off just taking their chances in getting sold off. Perhaps freedom had too big a price.

Jeremiah had a way with words, though. He did his best to describe the rising strength of the abolitionist movement in the North. By the late 1850s the movement had changed its tactics from that of bewailing the horrors of slavery to inciting open aggression against all of slavery's proponents. Indeed, the more radical abolitionists were already arming the Negroes and filling their heads with the glories to be gained from insurrection. The underground railroad, insisted Jeremiah, was one of the least violent of the various antislavery campaigns.

Jim took it all in and then decided he would simply have to trust those northern benefactors, who for some unfathomable reason had chosen to take up the cause of the southern slave. What of Ben and Nell, though? Should he tell them before they continued this journey how precariously their lives hung in the balance? Did they know that each person who helped them, whether black or white, was risking terrible retribution? Should he tell them the hard, cold facts, that even in the North they would not be loved, because their skin was black? The more he thought of these things, the less inclined he was to share them with the young couple.

Glancing down at the pair huddled under the old sailcloth, Jim felt a pang of reminiscence for his own lost loves and forgotten dreams. No point, he decided, in telling them how tight this was going to be. Instead, he braced himself against the wind and headed farther out to sea.

Master Weldon had spent several days shopping in Beaufort. There had been increasing talk of a slave rebellion, and he decided that he must do more in the way of protecting his family. Gilly was old enough now to have come along, but the father in Gilbert Weldon recoiled at the thought of putting further fear into his son's mind. In his own way Gilbert loved the Negroes under his care. They were "his people," and he didn't want his son to see them any differently. He liked the relationship that had developed between Gilly and Zach, and nothing pleased him more than the close affection his son felt toward Maum Beezie and Gullah Jim. Those three blacks were a real prize, there was no doubt about it!

Actually, Gilbert didn't believe there would be a slave uprising—not here on the Sea Islands anyway. The Gullah folk on these islands were treated well. Unlike the slaves in the other cotton lands of the South, the Gullah people had been allowed to maintain their own culture, and, to some extent, their own language.

Look at his own people, thought Gilbert. There wasn't a rebellious one in the lot. Even that young buck Cudjo, who had given the overseer such a fit coming down from Charleston, was settling right in. As of late he had even made some downright intelligent suggestions on how to improve the production of the place. It certainly was gratifying to know that as a master, he was such a success! Nevertheless, Master Weldon returned home to Coosaw with two vicious-looking horse pistols and a sleek saber that balanced well in his hands. He felt terribly pleased with himself.

The turmoil, however, hit him within a few hours of his return, and his self-satisfaction quickly faded. A delegation of planters from the St. Helena patrol came over by boat to hold an earnest discussion with the owner of Weldon Oaks. They were still feeling the effects of the night before. Indeed, they had returned to their homes well after midnight, wet and cold from a thwarted search, only to be disturbed by the rumble of the drums well into the wee hours of the morning. Those black devils were planning an insurrection, and that was for certain! This recent escape was surely only the beginning of their troubles.

Old Mr. Driscoll was normally a soft-spoken man, but his face turned hard, and his voice grew angry as he told Gilbert of the events of the previous night. "There's been a plot brewing, Weldon, right under our noses. Those two slaves didn't do this on their own. We reckon there's a whole chain of conspirators. They've been holding secret meetings at their praying grounds. Got that straight from my slave driver, Daniel."

Harry Martin broke in, gesturing angrily as he talked. "These secret night meetings have to be stopped. Praying grounds, bah! It ain't religion that they're singin' and stompin' about out there. One of my bucks finally came clean after a bit of persuasion. They were singin' their spirituals all right— somethin' about goin' down to the sea—but it wasn't Moses they was referin' to, no sir. That was nothin' more'n a secret code. They were hatchin' themselves an escape route and beatin' their drums half the night to let the rest of them shiftless devils know what was comin' off. Next thing ya know, they'll be plannin' themselves a real insurrection. If ya ask me, we best arm ourselves to the teeth!"

Master Weldon gave them a perplexed look. "But I've had no indication of such goings on over here on Coosaw. I treat my people well, Harry. I've never had anyone try to escape, and I'm certainly not expecting any uprisings. I'm sorry for the problems you're having." He hesitated, trying to keep the growing anger out of his voice. "But perhaps you've been too harsh with them, man. If there's insurrection brewing on your plantation, you've no one to blame but yourself. You're too quick to use that whip, Harry."

Harry's face turned a mottled red. "Listen here, Weldon, I'm in no mood for your opinions on how to deal with my slaves. Those fool dogs dragged us half the length of St. Helena and over every bramble patch on Ladies Island last night. And ya know where the trail ended? Right out there at the crossing point to Coosaw!"

"Are you trying to tell me that those two fugitives are here on Coosaw?" Gilbert looked stunned.

Mr. Driscoll lifted his hands for silence. "No, they're not on Coosaw," he said firmly. "We spotted them, all right, and we would have caught them too. But before we could get close enough to grab them, this little sprit-rigged bateau came flying out of the darkness, scooped them up, and beat it back out onto the river. We could barely get a shot off."

"That's right, Weldon," spat Harry, "scooped 'em up like he knew just where they were all along. And we've been figurin' that we know who it is who owns that bateau."

"Just what are you trying to say, Harry?"

"I'm sayin' that we want to talk to that old Nigra fisherman of yours, Weldon. You and your 'proper treatment' of slaves! You've been too lenient with that old man. Turn him over to me, and I'll get the truth out of him!"

Four-year-old Laura May, hiding in her secret spot on the top landing of the stairs, watched Papa's back go rigid. Her breath caught sharply in her throat, for she sensed his anger, though she could not understand its cause.

Gilly, hearing the commotion in the front parlor, joined his younger sister on the landing. "What's going on, Laura? What's all the shouting about?"

"Don't know," answered the little girl truthfully, her chin beginning to quiver. "Those men are awfully mad at Papa, Gilly. 'Sides, I don't think they like Mister Gullah Jim very much either." That's what she always called the old black fisherman, for somehow to her young mind, he needed the extra title.

Gilly, of course, knew far more about Papa's close relationship with Gullah Jim than Laura May did. The old man was his favorite. When just a boy like himself, Papa had spent many a happy hour with the old black fishing on the river and hunting through the woods of the outer islands. Jim was never just a slave; he was an elderly companion, a teacher in the manly arts of fishing and hunting. More than that—he was a friend. And now it was he, Gilly, who was learning the ways of boats and the sea from Gullah Jim. It was the kind of knowledge that no Sea Islander should be without, and Gilly could have no better instructor.

The angry questioning went on, and Gilly waited breathlessly for Papa's reply. Laura May had buried her face in the sleeve of his shirt, afraid to watch, but like him, unable to leave.

Papa's voice, when it came, was cold and hard. "I'm afraid that you've made a mistake, gentlemen. If there's a conspiracy to steal your slaves, I suggest you look elsewhere. I've just recently come from Harbor Island to pick up some provisions. Gullah Jim and I went out there two days ago to do some hunting. He was with me all of last night. As a matter of fact, he's still over there now, waiting for my return."

Gilly turned and looked at Laura May questioningly. What was Papa talking about? He hadn't been to Harbor Island at all; he'd gone into Beaufort and returned only that morning.

"I'm sorry for your troubles, gentlemen," continued Papa, his voice still as hard as flint. "Someone must have stolen that bateau several days ago. Jim and I had to take my own skiff over to the island. We would appreciate your letting us know, however, if you find his boat. She was a well-built craft, and Jim would hate to lose her."

With great politeness Gilbert showed the men to the door. They left in sullen silence, their mission having come to another dead end. After they had gone, he turned and looked toward the landing, catching the startled gaze of his two children. Then turning on his heel, he walked into the library and shut the door behind him with a resounding thud.

Gilly was astounded by what he had witnessed. Never before had the thought come to him that his father might be anything less than perfect. But there on the landing, with his own ears, he had heard Papa tell a bald-faced lie! In a strange sort of way, the thought unnerved him. Yet what else could Papa have done? If it were true—if Gullah Jim had indeed helped the slave couple to escape—he could be hanged without even the semblance of a trial.

A week later the broken remains of the bateau were found on the beach of Pritchards Island, just a short distance beyond the mouth of Fripp's Inlet. Gilly went with Jim by dugout canoe to recover the wreckage. An old sailcloth lay tangled amongst the pile of torn rigging and broken cedar boards. "Me-oh-my," said Jim, shaking his head sadly as he surveyed the wreck. "Sure was a purty little boat in she day. Gwanna have ta build we a new one right soon."

10

Down by de Riberside

(1857)

It was spring again. This time, however, the joy of the season was muted by cold rains and heavy winds. The fields, when not flooded, were filled with mud, and the plowing of the cotton grounds went slowly. None of the hands wanted to work outdoors in such miserable weather, but it was mid-March, and the planting must be done soon, or there would be no cotton crop this season.

Sickness ran rampant in the quarters. Maum Beezie fell into bed each night too tuckered out to eat her own supper. The mistress had excused her from the big house, knowing that without the old woman's nursing skills they would lose more people than they could afford to replace.

Old and young were equally affected. Besides the usual illnesses such as coughs and colds, there were dysentery, worms, lockjaw, and pneumonia. The last of these was the greatest killer of slaves. Planters found it entirely impractical to keep their field hands warm and dry simply because they had come down with a chest cold. And with no medicines to treat the insidious lung infections, little could be done other than to make the patient comfortable during his last hours of life.

Maum Beezie thought about this as she walked down the wooded path toward the quarters. She carried a small bottle

129

containing the grains of a blue powderlike substance. The master had handed it to her that very morning, insisting that she give Jeremiah a good dose as soon as possible. Having purchased the medication from a Beaufort physician some months earlier, the master now kept it on hand for the personal use of his family.

Slaves were rarely accorded the privilege of store-bought drugs, and this willingness on the part of Master Weldon to share the precious powder indicated how much he held the old groom in esteem. Normally the bottle was kept locked in the small wooden chest in the master's bedroom; prescription drugs were hard to come by and were much valued. The name of the medicine and the indications for its use were plainly written in a neat hand on the bottle's label. "POWDERED MERCURY," it said, "To improve and increase the secretions of the body." It was a favorite drug of the time and was often used to reduce fevers and fend off pneumonia.

Maum Beezie looked at the bottle dubiously. She had no great faith in white doctors, and she especially mistrusted their often-painful treatments and strong medicines. But she had tried everything else to cure Jeremiah—every root and herb that she knew.

Her husband lay in their one-room cabin back in the quarters, his body as wasted and dry as the Spanish-moss stuffing in the mattress beneath him. His illness had started with a head cold and then gone into a persistent cough. As his cough progressed with intensity, Jeremiah was often left too weak and shaky to perform his duties well. But he was persistent and tried to hide his discomfort. This, of course, only made things worse.

The day finally came when he collapsed onto the muddy ground of the east paddock after a hard morning of mucking out the stalls. They had to carry him back to the cabin in the quarters, and Maum Beezie was summoned from the big house. One look told her that Jeremiah's days were numbered.

As she walked, Maum Beezie rubbed her thumb across the bottle's label and wondered how much of a dose she should give—a teaspoon, a tablespoon—and how many times a day? She couldn't read, and the master had given her no clues. And if it didn't work, what then? She must brace herself for the inevitable.

The woods were damp and smelled of earth and decaying leaves. But, scanning the ground with practiced eyes, Maum Beezie was struck by the signs of new life. Small green heads pushed through the carpet of pine needles and dead leaves. Maum Beezie stopped to touch a few of these and to talk to them gently.

It was the elderly woman's belief that all forms of life, even the smallest of plants, had the power to speak and to hear. Their voices were not human, of course. These little sprouts, for example, conversed with each other as they lay in the cradle of the earth. "Shall we poke out our heads and have a peek?" they would ask.

Then one, braver than the others, would do just that: "The sun is warm, and the air is fresh with spring rains. Come out and join me." Maum Beezie liked to imagine that she heard their chatter.

In an open spot at the side of the trail, a hoary-headed thistle was lifting its face to the sky. Other than a pale green, there was little color to its flower as yet, but the leaves and the large bud were already bristling with a dangerous spray of sharp needles. How odd, thought the old woman, that even among the plants there was this effort for self-defense. With plants like the thistle, the threat was real; in others, however, it was simply a sham.

What of Jeremiah, she wondered? What were his self-defenses? Was it his faith in a merciful God and the promise of a better hereafter—or was that simply for show? Had he used his powers of speech and persuasion to cover his own doubts, or did he truly believe that his people would one day find freedom? In any case, she decided, his personal battle would soon be over, and in that there was mercy.

Tucking the bottle into the pocket of her apron, she moved down the trail as fast as her rheumatic legs would carry her.

When she reached the cabin, she found a small crowd gathered. The people, their faces lined with concern, stood in a tight little cluster and talked in small, whispering sounds.

Upon seeing the old plantation nurse, a woman named Suky turned to face her. "It's de witch what's been riddin' he. Stand on he chest and suck out he breath," she said with a trembling voice. "Po' ol' Jeremiah don' hab de strength ta push her off."

Then another, an old man this time, elbowed his way forward and wanted to be heard. "No witch dis time, Suky; no hag needder. Hags 'n witches hain't strong 'nough ta bring down a righteous man like Jeremiah." Dropping his voice to a whisper, he confided that he knew for certain it was conjuring that had placed the groom in such a terrible state. "I's gwanna bring you a ruffle hen. Ruffle hen peck 'round de yard an' find dat conju bag what ben hid."

Maum Beezie listened to each one of them patiently. They meant well. They, too, were searching for some way to help this man who had led them from the dark valleys of life as they knew it to the spiritual hilltops. His passing would leave them without hope.

The cabin felt damp and musty when she entered it. Not a healthy place to die, she thought sadly. She wished she had another window, that a shaft of sunlight would break through the shadowed doorway.

Jeremiah seemed to be resting comfortably now, although his breathing was short and shallow. Laying her head against his chest, she could hear the rattling within. Should she awaken him and try to get a spoonful of the medicine down?

Just then, there was a shuffling sound in the corner. Moving her head quickly, Maum Beezie spied little Angel curled up on a mat near the fireplace. The child's crutches were beside her. Dear old Jeremiah. He had made those crutches for his granddaughter with his own hands and then patiently taught her to pull herself along on them.

Angel's gait had been stiff and awkward at first, but with practice she'd improved. How proud her grandpa had been when she finally stood erect and hobbled toward him, her little crutches thumping against the hard-packed dirt floor with a slow but steady rhythm. "Me-oh-my, chil', look how tall you be! Like a bean sprout fer ce'tain."

Angel had laughed at that. She always laughed when she was with Jeremiah. She'd climb on his knee and look deeply into his grizzled old face. Then she'd tug at his sleeve and ask in her gentle little voice, "Please, Grampa, sing de song 'bout heaben."

He would start out the song, his bass voice deep with emotion, for he loved the words as dearly as his granddaughter did:

> Good Lawd, in de manshans above,
> Good Lawd, in de manshans above,
> My Lawd, I hope ta meet my Jesus
> In de man-shans above.

"Now you sing de chorus wid me, honey," he'd say, and their voices would rise in beautiful harmony:

> If you get ta heaben befor' I do,
> Lawd tell my Jesus I'm comin' too,
> Ta de man-shans above.

A tear ran down the old woman's cheek. How was she ever going to tell this dear child that her grandpa was on his way to the mansion above?

There was a sound from the bed—a raspy cough, and then a weak voice calling her name. "Beezie, honey—you dere?"

"Yes, suh, Jeremiah. I's right here aside you."

"Won't be long now—glad I's goin', dough. Dis ol' world ain't as purty as when we was young."

"Ain't dat de trut', Jeremiah."

"Take care ob Angel. She be a good chil'."

"Dat's de trut', too, Jeremiah." Maum Beezie was having trouble speaking. Something kept catching in her throat, and her eyes were all misty.

Jeremiah moved his hands up to his chest and struggled to look down at them. "Dese hands done a lot ob work in dey day, Beezie."

"Um-hum."

"Done a lot ob prayin' too."

"Yes, Lawd. Yes, Lawd."

Reaching out, the old woman wrapped her gnarled hands around her husband's. Her tears dropped onto his chest and made little wet spots on his nightshirt. Jeremiah's lips were moving, but she could no longer hear the words. "Yes, Lawd. Yes, Lawd," she kept saying.

Then Angel was beside her. How had the child moved so quietly? Looking down, Maum Beezie was startled to see that Angel was without her crutches. Her little face was wet with tears.

"Grampa's goin' ta de manshans above, ain't he?" she said in a tiny voice.

"Yes, Lawd. Yes, Lawd," answered Maum Beezie.

When Master Weldon entered the cabin, he found them there together. Jeremiah's breath no longer came in shallow, rasping sounds. His chest was still; his hands were folded in prayer. The old slave was at peace.

Now the drumbeats were long and slow—a pause—and another slow roll. A line of sorrowful people moved toward the cabin under the tall loblolly pines. The sun was setting; the western sky was red and gold, with long wisps of lavender clouds radiating outward toward the blue zenith above.

From far and near they came, walking slowly, their bodies swaying and their heads bowed. It was time for Jeremiah's "settin'-up" service. He lay on his bed, his body clothed in one of the master's old suits. A shiny penny rested on each of his eyelids, and on his stomach lay a small pile of salt. His walking stick was beside him. According to custom, before closing the pine casket, the stick would be laid across the old man's chest so his spirit would have some familiar object and thus feel at rest.

One by one the people shuffled up to Jeremiah and placed

their hands on his remains to say goodbye. It comforted them to know that they had done this last act of kindness for the man whom they so deeply respected.

Suky was the last person in the long line of mourners to say goodbye, but when she reached the inert form of Jeremiah, her superstitious fears got the better of her. Placing the palms of her hands first on his mouth and then his ears, she said in a whisper, "Jeremiah, you hear we talkin'? Don't come back 'n haunt po' ol' Suky now. She ain't ready ta go wid you jes yet."

Gilly heard the woman and was amused by her words. For the time being, however, he was far more curious about how the body had been laid out.

"What's that pile of salt doing on Jeremiah's stomach?" he asked his father, trying to keep his voice low.

Papa leaned close to Gilly's ear. "To keep the stomach from purging," he answered.

"Oh." Now Gilly's interest was really pricked. At first he hadn't wanted to come to this "settin'-up" service, but now he was glad that his father had insisted.

The Gullah folk sat in a circle around the bed. They would stay here for the entire night to keep Jeremiah's spirit company. Only once, when the plantation carpenter came in with a string to measure the body, was the circle broken. The sound of hammering could now be heard from the yard; Jeremiah's final resting place would soon be ready.

Gilly's eyes searched the familiar cabin. There were dishes of food placed here and there on the crude bits of furniture, and to his surprise, there were also many broken plates and pieces of pottery.

Not wanting to disturb Papa again, Gilly turned toward Zach, who stood just behind him. He pointed to the dishes and broken pottery and lifted his eyebrows questioningly.

Zach's eyes were as wide as dinner plates, the whites showing plainly in contrast to his dark face. Without moving his head, he shifted his eyeballs first one way and then the other. Then he grimaced as though he had seen a ghost.

Gilly tried not to laugh, but he could barely hold it in.

Keeping his hand low to his side, he reached back and poked Zach in the stomach. The black boy let out his breath with a grunt. Slowly, walking sideways with tiny steps, the boys managed to make their way to the door.

"What you doin', Massa Gilly, poking we in de stomach like-a-dat? Don' you got no re-spect fer de daid?"

Gilly let out his breath with a short laugh, then clapped his hand over his mouth and pulled his face into a serious frown. "Sure I do. But I ain't never seen anything as strange as that in my whole life. What's that food sitting all over the place for? And how come they got broken dishes and chunks of pottery everywhere?"

"It's de custom."

"But why?"

Zach sat down on the door stoop and scratched his head. "Le'see now, I disremember, 'xactly de details, but et's sumpin' 'bout de sp'rit ob de daid pusson."

"Com'on, Zach! Of course, you can remember."

Zach scanned the yard carefully before he spoke. "Well, suh, be disaway. Daid pusson's sp'rit be still waitin' 'round durin' de settin'-up service. Get might hongry all dat time an' start lookin' fer sumpin' ta eat. Effen nobody hab food out fer she, dat sp'rit get right o'nery."

Gilly nodded in understanding.

"Now de broke-up dishes be unnuda t'ing. Dat's done ta break de chain."

"What chain?"

"De chain ob de fambly. Break de dishes so odder folks in de fambly not die."

It was evening again before the burial service commenced. Having no other spiritual leader to say words at the graveside, Master Weldon agreed to lead the service. He walked at the head of the procession, a torchbearer on either side of him. The rough pine coffin with Jeremiah's remains followed, carried on a cart drawn by the plantation's old Gray. A few paces behind the coffin were Maum Beezie and Angel, and beside them Gilly and Laura May. Master Weldon insisted that his children take part in the service as a sign of respect for the old man who had been in his service for so many years.

Walking in the families' wake was a long line of Negroes, many of whom carried brightly lighted torches. They walked two by two, swaying from side to side and singing one of the funeral dirges so well known on the Sea Islands:

> When I can read my title clear
> Ta mansions in de skies,
> I bid farewell to ev'ry fear
> An' wipe my weepin' eyes.

The procession moved slowly through the woods from the quarters, then turned in the direction of the river. On its bank was the slave cemetery, the open grave awaiting yet another departed member of the small plantation community. As was the custom, Jeremiah was laid to rest with his head to the west and his feet to the east. That way, when Gabriel blew his trumpet, he'd be facing in the right direction.

"Yes, suh, Massa Gilly. Bery impo'tant, bery impo'tant indeed. Dey mus' always face de east," explained Zach. "I knowd 'bout one time back home de massa bury dis po' ol' woman in de wrong direction. Next night eberybody sneak out, dig she up, set she in de right direction."

The two boys' tendency toward rowdiness had been tempered considerably since last night's settin'-up service. Perhaps it was the reality of the gaping hole in the earth that sobered them now. Gilly kept thinking back to all of those times when the old groom had walked beside him as he learned to ride Nutmeg. Similar thoughts went through Zach's mind, but added to them was the common bond of slavery that man and boy had each had to deal with in his own way.

The drums beat out a slow, dirgelike roll as the coffin was lowered into the grave. Following an ancient African custom, Gullah Jim leaned down and picked up Jeremiah's little granddaughter. Willing arms on the other side of the grave reached out for Angel, and she was passed over her grandfather's coffin.

"Dat's so de sp'rit don' come back an' haunt de chil'," explained Zach under his breath. Gilly felt rather sorry for the little black girl; although she was no longer crying, she looked frightened to death.

Papa said his words over the grave, then read a text from the big Bible that was usually kept on the reading table in the front parlor. As the service came to a close, the people each took a handful of dirt and dropped it onto the coffin. Then, as the pine box disappeared, the people sang one last mournful song:

> Hark! From de tomb a doleful soun'
>   My ears attend de cry;
> Ye libin' men, come view de ground
>   Where you must shortly lie.

It was over. Jeremiah was gone. Only one task remained, and that was to place on top of the packed mound of earth an array of his possessions: his favorite bowl, a large wooden spoon, an old alarm clock that had been given to him by the master, and the lantern he used to light his way to the stable on those winter mornings when he arose before the sun. Each item was carefully placed so the spirit would not miss these special belongings and come searching for them through the quarters during the dark of night.

Whether Jeremiah would have approved of customs that undoubtedly had pagan origins was never a concern. It was the way things had been done for generations, as far back as anyone could remember. But mixed in with these ancient practices were more recent ones. Many who left the lonely graveyard by the side of the river remembered these as they walked through the dark woods back to their cabins.

The old groom had never had the privilege of owning a Bible, nor could he read. Like most of the Gullah folk, however, he had an excellent memory. When Jeremiah spoke from the Word, it was as though his listeners heard the very voice of the Lord. His mourners remembered this now, and in their minds they heard once again the text that their beloved spiritual leader had treasured above all others:

> They that wait upon the Lord,
> Shall renew their strength;
> They shall mount up with wings as eagles;
> They shall run, and not be weary;
> And they shall walk, and not faint (Isaiah 40:31).

11
Stay in de Fields

(1860)

Samuel lifted the hoe and brought it down hard by the small stake that marked the end of his second task of ground. The force of the movement sent a cloud of dust into his face, coating his tongue and the insides of his nostrils with a powder-dry sand. He blew his nose into his ragged shirt sleeve and then worked up a mouthful of saliva and spat it out forcefully. Surely this spring heat wave must break soon.

It had been a week of windless days, unusual for the Sea Islands. Now the sun, like the brass disc of a Chinese gong, hung high in the western sky. The afternoon was half-gone, but the heat would linger until well past sunset.

Despite the oppressive weather, Samuel had done twice his share of work. He was tired but felt pride in knowing that he was a "two-task" man. Few of the other field hands could match him for speed and strength. Young Daniel over there, even with his muscular build, could barely finish one task of ground with a full day's work. But then, the boy was big for his age. His arms, having grown faster than the rest of his body, threw him off balance.

With his master's work finished, Samuel moved into the shade of a pecan tree and called for the water boy. He dipped his hands into the lukewarm water and splashed his face. Then he straightened up, stretched the kinks from his back, and surveyed the day's accomplishments. Samuel knew that most men his size, if they were good, could list a task and a half a day. It was satisfying to know that he was better than "good."

Across the field he could see Cudjo talking to three young bucks. "Dat pack ob vermin!" he muttered under his breath. "When de buzzards circlin', sumpin' rotten layin' in de ditch fer certain."

Lifting a clod of dirt, Samuel crushed it between his large hands. Slave driver, indeed! There was no better title for Cudjo. To those who did not serve his ambitious purposes, he was an unrelenting taskmaster. If given half the chance to use a whip, he would have applied it with a vengeance. Not so, however, with the chosen few who followed his lead. The slave driver was blind to their laziness. Working up another mouthful of saliva, Samuel spat it onto the ground. Why, if Cudjo and his pack of jackals spent half as much time working as they did leaning on their hoes, this field would have been planted two weeks ago!

For a slave, Samuel was an unusual sort. If he could have been his own man, he would have moved heaven and earth to get a piece of land. He felt satisfaction in turning over the sod, planting the seed, and watching new life stretch toward the sun. He only needed to look at a plot of ground to understand why a planter would choose to keep a plow from it. The Low Country was covered with the silt run-off of the high, western lands. Furrowing it deep with a plow blade would disrupt the balance. It would mix the poor subsoil with the rich loam of the surface, thereby lessening the fertility of the whole.

Samuel spat onto the tips of his fingers and ran his thumb along the sharp blade of his hoe. There was a heap of work a determined man like himself could do. If he had his own piece of ground, he wouldn't need much in the way of tools—a good hoe like this and maybe an ax. A mule would be nice but not necessary. He kicked at the dirt with his bare toes, noting with satisfaction that there were no stones. Why should a man try to dig out what was not there in the first place? No, a plow and mule would not be necessary—not at first.

All of this went through Samuel's mind as he stood beneath the pecan tree and surveyed the wide expanse of fields lying open to the cloudless sky. He was so occupied with his thoughts that he failed to hear the approach of the overseer.

"Well, boy, looks like you done a fair piece of work again today."

Samuel spun around and slumped his shoulders, remembering that pride wasn't becoming in a slave. "Ye'suh, Mr. Ned, I try ma best."

"Rare thing to see in a man whose sweat and blood belong to another."

Samuel was surprised to hear the overseer echo his own thoughts. He took no offense; the words had not been meant as a taunt.

"Mayhap, Mr. Ned."

Walking to the water bucket, the overseer ladled out a dipperful and lifted it toward his mouth. He stopped in midair, the dipper spilling water. His eyes riveted hard on Cudjo and narrowed. "Blast that conniving . . . !" Throwing the ladle back into the bucket with disgust, the overseer pounded his fist into his hand. "Driver! You think we're holding a tea party out here?" he shouted angrily. "Get those hands back to work and make it quick, or I'll have your hide nailed to the barn!"

Cudjo lifted his head slowly and stared at the overseer, his face a study of haughty superiority. Several seconds passed before he lifted his hand and casually waved his men back to work.

Samuel felt uncomfortable. He wanted to move away, distance himself from the scene, but such an action might implicate him in Cudjo's boldness. Instead, he examined the ground and tried to keep his face impassive. Why, he wondered, was the overseer letting a black man, driver or no, get away with such impudence?

Wiping his mouth with the back of his hand, the overseer cleared his throat and spat onto the ground. "Bad taste in my mouth," he said, to no one in particular.

Samuel decided to use the slave's best defense and feign ignorance. He scratched his head, wiped the sweaty streaks of dirt from his cheeks with the cuff of his sleeve, and casually slung the hoe over his shoulder. Shuffling a bit so as to kick up a small dust cloud at his feet, he approached the overseer and tipped his straw hat respectfully. "Mr. Ned, suh, be mighty 'bliged effen I kin mobe 'long now."

The overseer spun around and surveyed Samuel with narrowed eyes and then pulled his mouth into a lopsided grin. "Don't rush off, boy. I got sumpin' to discuss with you."

Apprehension crept into Samuel's mind. Considering the overseer's bad humor, he'd just as soon be somewhere else. But the tone of the man's voice had changed, and Samuel's curiosity was aroused.

"Like I said, boy, you do good work." Ned rubbed his bulbous nose hard with the back of his hand. He wasn't used to passing out compliments to anyone, let alone a common field hand.

"The fact is," he began and then sniffed hard, "the master has the right to expect a good day's work 'cause, most times leastways, he treats his people fair." There was a pause while Ned glanced over his shoulder at Cudjo. Then muttering under his breath, he added, "Unless some ignoramus puts a bug in his ear."

Samuel thought this over. Perhaps the man was right. Not every planter would allow a slave to have part of the day as his own when his assigned tasks were done. "Ye'suh, Mr. Ned," he answered. "Massa be mighty good man."

The overseer was staring hard at Cudjo's back. "Glad you feel that way, Sam," he said slowly as he scratched at the stubble on his chin. "Got me a plan buzzin' round in my head. Been thinking about going to the master—askin' him to make you a driver." Without turning his head, he shifted his eyes toward Samuel. "Now that'd put one over on that uppity nigger, wouldn't it?"

Samuel was startled. He found himself straightening up,

feeling a bit taller—more like a man. Then, getting hold of his better sense, he forced his frame back into a dejected slump.

"*No, suh*, Mr. Ned. Don' wants ta be no driber man." He accentuated his slow, stumbling speech. "Like de land, sho 'nough, but dis po' ol' nigger ain't got what it takes ta make udder folks work 'gainst dere wills."

Samuel cringed. Had he said too much? The overseer might be a bit backward, but he was no fool. Was it possible for him to look past the mask of demeaned stupidity and see the anger and resentment that boiled just under the surface? Examining the man's eyes carefully, Samuel breathed a sigh of relief. His words had evidently been taken at face value.

"That's the difference between you and the rest of the hands, Sam. Now take that Cudjo, for instance; he don't care a penny for his own people. And them three bucks he's been jawin' with—huh—he ain't pulled the wool over my eyes on that score. Why, he's got them vermin believin' that he's Nat Turner come back from the dead! No good'll come from that, I'll tell ya!"

Not sure if he was meant to respond to the last remark, Samuel lifted his head sideward and glanced up at the overseer's face. Of course, he understood about Nat Turner, though it was something a slave who valued his skin would never admit to. As near as Samuel could figure, Turner, who had been a black preacher some thirty years ago, held a considerable piece of influence with his fellow slaves. Some thought of him as a type of messiah, divinely ordained to lead his people to freedom. One hardly had to be told the outcome of that idea—it was all too predictable. After a bloody rebellion, Turner and his followers, for all of their high ideals, had ended up swinging from a gibbet.

"You ain't afraid of that no count Cudjo, are you, boy?"

The overseer's question startled Samuel from his thoughts. "No, suh, Mr. Ned. Cudjo mo' wind den stom."

The overseer turned sharply and faced Samuel. "Listen to me good, boy. I reckon you care about your people leastwise half as much as you care about freedom. Hey, you think maybe I was born yesterday? There's fire in your eyes, boy. Despite all that, 'yes, suh,' 'no, suh,' 'don't neber no mind, suh,' stuff, you got a few pieces of brain left in your head. Now if you can just get up some gumption, you might be able to save these people from a lot of unpleasantness."

Samuel stood silently surveying the overseer's face. He wasn't exactly sure what the man was leading up to. There was one thing for certain, however; becoming a slave driver was no way to get in good with his fellow field hands.

Ned's voice rattled on relentlessly. "Let 'em know how things stand. Let 'em know exactly what's at the end of that glory road Cudjo's been talking about."

Samuel felt a trickle of sweat roll down his spine. The overseer's face was close to his. He could smell the man's foul breath, but he dared not turn away. Dark, uneven whiskers blotched Ned's chin and stood out like the bristles of a pig. The dirty nail of his index finger poked hard at Samuel's chest. His words were accompanied by occasional flecks of spittle that shot out from between the gaps in his teeth and spattered the black man's face.

"The master hasn't seen the light yet, but the time'll come—mark my words—the time'll come when he does. As for you, boy, you best pray that it ain't too late, either."

"Don't rightly understand you, Mr. Ned."

"Come on, Sam, don't play dumb with me. You don't fool me no mor'n Cudjo does. Both of you are as sly as foxes— only with Cudjo, it's the devil himself what's doin' all the thinking."

Samuel pulled his neck down into his collar. This sort of talk scared him. The overseer, for all his tough words and uncouth manners, had a way of looking into a man's head. Up until now he'd been simply beating around the bush, but Samuel had the feeling that he was about to get down to the real purpose of this conversation.

Ned scratched the back of his neck and then examined his fingernails as he talked. "Well, boy, if the idea of being a slave driver don't suit you none, I 'spect there's something else that would. As a matter of fact, the way I see it, you was downright born for it."

Samuel waited patiently.

"I been noticing how all the hands look up to you, Sam. They got a question, they come to you. They got a complaint, you're the first one who'll listen. More'n once I seen you quiet things down when trouble was about to brew." He waited for a response, but receiving none, rushed on. "Let me put it like this; if you should take yourself off to see the master this evenin', wouldn't be me who'd hinder you."

"What I wanna see de massa fo', Mr. Ned?"

"Boy, if you ain't stupid, which you ain't, you certainly are slow! Look out in those fields. See how them hands are moppin' around like the sky's about to fall on 'em? You think it's just 'cause they gotta hoe a few rows of cotton?"

Samuel scanned the field with a perplexed look. He couldn't see a thing different about the field hands than he'd seen every other day of his life.

"Must be the sun that's tetched your head, boy!" The overseer's voice was growing louder, and several of the people working nearby turned to look at him in wonder. "They've lost their preacher man! They ain't got nobody to tell 'em that, if they keep on keepin' on, the day of glory hallelujah is sure to come."

Samuel turned startled eyes on the overseer. "Wa's dat got ta do wid me?" he asked.

For an answer, the overseer slapped his forehead with the heel of his hand. "Maybe you *are* just stupid, after all!"

Samuel spent the remainder of the afternoon fishing on the banks of the Coosaw River. It was a good feeling to lie idle in the sun, listening to the clacking mating calls of the fiddler crabs and the steady buzz of insects. The sun was low in the western sky when he finally pushed himself upright and headed back to the quarters.

Samuel was so busy with thoughts of what the overseer had

said that he nearly failed to notice the dozen or so oarsmen lounging on the warm planks of the dock. When he did see them, he was surprised by the array of skiffs and bateaux tied to the moorings. "Massa must habe a passel ob comp'ny," he said to himself.

His guess was confirmed when he reached the trail that ran just below the lawns of the big house. On the lower deck of the piazza sat a row of planters from St. Helena's and its surrounding islands. They were engaged in a heated discussion. One, a tall man whose voice carried better than the others, was on his feet pounding the piazza railing with his fist. "States' rights! States' rights! That's what the constitution guarantees. I'm sick to death of them northern abolitionists and rabble-rousers tellin' us about the evils of slavery. Why, they'd have us parceling out land and setting up housekeeping for every slave in the South. You don't see them scrambling all over each other to do it in their own states, now, do you?"

Samuel tried to act oblivious to all the ruckus, but there was something about the man's intensity that made him prick up his ears. Feigning a thorn in his foot, he leaned against a tree trunk and made believe that he was trying to dig it out.

A heavyset man with a mottled red face was now on his feet. "That fellow Townsend is as right as rain," he shouted. "I've read every word the man's written. It all boils down to this: Slavery is absolutely essential to the southern economy. Why, without slave labor, we'd be ruined in a year. Let me tell you, gentlemen, if we intend to maintain our present quality of life, we've got to take some strong measures. They've forced our hand. Secession from the Union is the only answer!"

There was a loud murmur from the assembled company. Samuel didn't recognize the next speaker, but he had a commanding way about him that made the rest of the planters quiet down to listen. Walking to the head of the stairs, the tall, white-haired man planted his hands firmly on his hips and cleared his throat. His voice, when it came, carried loud and clear across the wide lawns. "I say that if the rest of the southern states can't get up the nerve to secede, South Carolina should show 'em how it's done!"

There was a loud shout of approval; every man was on his feet now, each one trying to be heard above the other. Try as he might, Samuel caught nothing more of what was being said. He'd heard enough, however. There were changes in the wind—*big* changes. He felt an odd thrill of excitement, as if something good was just around the bend. Somewhere out there were a passel of folks who wanted to do away with slavery. Maybe—just maybe . . .

The quarters were abuzz with activity when Samuel walked down the sandy street. The women stood over their large cook pots, stirring succulent-smelling stews with long-handled paddles. The menfolk busied themselves with their personal chores or lay on their porch stoops with the hope of getting a quick snooze before supper. Children were everywhere. Two little ones ran past Samuel rolling the hoop of an old whiskey barrel. A boy of about eight had a June bug tied to a piece of string and was watching the hapless insect as it beat its wings in a futile effort to escape. As Samuel approached his own cabin, he had to walk around a group of children who were dancing in a circle with their arms intertwined. They were playing one of the many ring games so popular with Gullah children. The games always involved a lot of singing, and if the participants really got into the spirit, a good deal of loud laughter.

For some reason Samuel was feeling terribly lonely this evening. He kept thinking of Phoebe and how wonderful life would have been if she had lived and become his wife. There was another young woman he'd had his eye on recently, and if he did go to the master about anything, perhaps it would be about her. But not yet. He wasn't ready for that just yet.

Suddenly feeling very tired, Samuel lay down on his bunk to rest. Try as he might, though, he couldn't sleep. The overseer's words kept going through his mind. What had the man been thinking of? Did he really expect a lowly field hand to stop a slave rebellion, if, in fact that's what Cudjo was plotting? And why should a slave rebellion be any of his concern? Though he wasn't particularly happy with his lot, the master *was* a fair man and provided well for his people.

The children must have moved closer to his cabin, for their voices came to him loudly now and drowned out his thoughts. Suddenly the words of their song struck him like a sledge hammer:

> We raise de wheat,
> Dey gib us de corn;
> We bake de bread,
> Dey gib us de crust;
> We sif' de meal,
> Dey gib us de huss;
> We peel de meat,
> Dey gib us de skin;

"Dat's right!"

Samuel surprised himself by saying the words out loud. Hadn't his people put up with as much misery as any one group of folk should ever have to take? But it couldn't be done in Cudjo's way; they'd only hurt themselves more, and a lot of innocent folk, black and white, would get bloodied in the process. The best way to . . .

No, he mustn't have such thoughts! They were dangerous; they made him want to do things that he'd worked hard to push to the back of his mind. Besides, he was tired. He needed his sleep if he wanted to complete more than one task tomorrow. How nice it would be to lie on the bank of the river again and think of nothing.

Rolling over in his bed and covering his ears with the pillow, Samuel tried to block out the voices of the children. But try as he might, he knew that he couldn't put a stop to the way his thoughts were moving.

The overseer was right; those people out there definitely needed some spiritual leadership. But not him—surely not him! He'd been through all of this just after Phoebe's funeral.

For a while it had seemed right, even enticing. But as time passed and the vision of gaining his freedom and owning a piece of land had grown in his mind, the other dream faded.

"No, Lawd!" he said out loud. "Not we. Fin' sumbody else." Negative arguments washed over him like the muddy waters of a turbulent flood. He had lost Phoebe, the one person who could have given him the courage to face such a challenge. Then he had compounded his loss by letting Cudjo make a fool of him at the funeral. The final cap on the issue, however, was his apparent poor memory. Why, he'd forgotten more than half the Scripture texts that poor old Jeremiah had taught him!

Samuel turned over in his bed and burrowed his head under his hands. Some preacher man he'd make if he couldn't even think of what to preach about! Besides, what was he getting himself all worked up for, anyhow? Anyone with half a brain knew it was the master who'd decide on the new Praise House Watchman. As far as Samuel could tell, the master didn't even know he existed.

Samuel's thoughts returned to his new dream. Someday, if he worked hard and learned all he could about the land and how to grow things. Well, he'd have to find a way to earn some money so he could buy his freedom. Then again, what if he worked so hard that his master, out of the goodness of his heart, decided to just set him free!

By this time the singers had gone on to another ditty. They were shouting out the words so loudly that some of the children had fallen to the ground. They rolled about under his window, laughing and giggling. Two of the youngest ones jumped onto his front stoop and kept up the beat by pounding their feet repeatedly against the wooden boards.

> My ol' missus promise me
>   Shoo a la a day,
> When she die she set me free,
>   Shoo a la a day,
> She live so long her head git bald,

Shoo a la a day.
  She give up de idea ob dyin' a-tall,
Shoo a la a day.

The loud knock on his door made Samuel sit up with a jerk. "Samuel, are you in there?"

Was it possible? It sounded like the master's son. Why would he be here in the slave quarters? Tightening the frayed rope that cinched up the waist of his trousers, Samuel walked to the door and opened it carefully. There, sure enough, stood Gilly, with his personal slave, Zach, standing just behind him.

"Excuse me, Samuel, I didn't mean to awaken you."

The young master had a polite way about him that made Samuel feel important. Motioning with his hand, he invited the two boys in. "What kin I do fer you, Massa Gilly?"

"Oh, it's not for me, Samuel," Gilly said as he looked around the small cabin with an unfeigned curiosity. Zach remained standing quietly in the background. "It's Papa who wants you. Said I should come down here myself to get you."

"Dere sumpin' wrong, Massa Gilly?" asked Samuel, as a sudden spark of fear shot through him.

"Not that I know of," answered the boy.

Zach stepped out of the shadows and smiled shyly at the big black man with the muscular arms and intelligent face. How he admired Samuel! "Mr. Samuel, suh, tain't a t'ing ta worry 'bout. De oberseer come up ta de big house dis ebenin' jes as all de St. Helena's folk be leabin'. Say he got sumpin' he want ta talk wid de massa 'bout."

Gilly punched Zach in the arm. "Hey! How come you know so much? You been spying again?"

Zach smiled crookedly at Gilly, and the two of them broke into laughter. Forgetting the purpose of their mission, they began pummeling each other playfully on the arms and chest. Samuel smiled despite himself, remembering his own boyhood. He liked the unassuming friendship the boys had developed for each other.

Samuel followed the boys up the path through the woods to the big house. The lawns were dark now, and the air was heady with the smell of night-blooming jasmine. They approached the front piazza, and Samuel could just make out the form of Maum Beezie sitting in a rocking chair. When they reached the top step, he realized that she held Laura May on one knee and Angel on the other. She'd been telling them bedtime stories, and their little faces fairly glowed with pleasure.

Stopping only long enough to smile knowingly at Samuel, the old woman commenced to rock and tell her stories.

"Den breh rabbit say ta breh wolf . . ."

Samuel followed Gilly and Zach into the wide foyer and down the hallway to the master's study. Master Weldon sat at a large mahogany desk. A stack of accounts and a large leather journal lay in front of him. He wore a velvet robe with a dark floral design that looked rich in the shadowed lamplight.

So this is how the white man lives, thought Samuel. It was so far removed from the cabins of the quarters that he could barely take it all in.

Samuel had never been in the big house before, let alone in the master's own study. He tried not to appear curious, but the opulent surroundings made him stare in open wonder. The master, sensing his awe, waited until Samuel had had his fill of looking.

"Have a seat." The master motioned to a high-backed chair with a plush seat cover. Samuel sat on its edge, acutely aware of his grubby work pants and dirty fingernails.

"Gilly, you might as well sit down too. It's about time you got some idea of how a plantation must be run."

Zach started to step out of the room, but Master Weldon called him back. "You may stay, Zach. What I've got to say to Samuel is hardly a secret, and it will significantly affect your people."

Zach sat down on a small window bench and tried to act nonchalant. He pulled up his legs and concentrated on the flicker of fireflies against the dark background of pines and live oaks.

"Well, Samuel," began the master, his voice suddenly very serious, "I guess you know why I've asked you to come."

Samuel could only look at him dumbly. He felt out of place, like a mule in the mistress's front parlor. His tongue didn't seem to fit in his mouth properly, and his hands felt too big for his arms. "No, suh, massah. Kyan't say dat I do."

The master smiled, and Samuel felt a bit more at ease. "I've been noticing the kind of work you've been doing, Samuel, and I'm right proud of you. The overseer tells me that you've got a way with the soil."

"Yes, suh, Massa Weldon. I likes de feel ob de groun'."

"He also tells me that you've got leadership qualities, that the people look up to you—that they come to you with their problems. He says that he's offered to make you a driver."

Samuel just shrugged. He was beginning to feel uncomfortable again. This chair might have a soft cushion, but it somehow didn't suit him.

"I believe that your answer was No. Is that correct?"

"Yes, suh. It were No, suh."

"Hmm, hard to understand, but if that's the way you want it . . ."

"Well, Samuel," continued the master, "I've got another idea, and before you say No, I want you to hear me out."

"Yes, suh, Massa Weldon."

"You know how much Jeremiah's loss is felt by the people— by me and my family too. He was a grand old man, and he kept this place together in more ways than one."

"Yes, suh, dat he was!"

"Jeremiah and I had the opportunity to talk some before he passed away. He told me that you had a quick mind and could memorize Scripture texts quite well."

Samuel tried to pull his head farther down into his collar. He could feel drops of sweat forming on his brow. He reached up clumsily and wiped them away, but now his neck and back felt sweaty too.

"I'm sure you also know that it's the master's responsibility to appoint the Praise House Watchman when the previous elder is gone." The master stood up and walked over to Samuel's chair. He looked down at him kindly and placed his hand on the big buck's shoulder. "This is a bit hard to explain, Samuel, but I'm afraid that there are some changes coming to this area—perhaps to the country as a whole. I know that you don't understand politics or government or anything like that." Master Weldon hesitated and then walked back to his desk and turned once more to face Samuel.

"No, suh. Don' know nothin' 'bout dat so'ta stuff."

"But you *do* know how to get your own people to respect you," shot back the master in one quick breath.

Samuel just shook his head. "Ain't neber t'ought ob t'ings data way," he answered quickly. The scene at Phoebe's grave-side was coming back all too vividly.

"Well, *they* do, Samuel. Both Gullah Jim and Maum Beezie have told me they do. Now listen here, my good fellow . . ."

Samuel couldn't help but notice that it was the master who was sweating now. He seemed uncomfortable, as though what he was trying to say was costing him some great effort.

"Hu-humm." Master Weldon cleared his throat loudly; his Adam's apple bobbed up and down. "The fact is, I—well, the fact is—I need you." Having gotten out those words, the rest came in a rush. "I really care about my people, Samuel, and I don't want anything bad happening to them. It's important that there's someone whom I can trust, someone to give them leadership—one of their own."

"Please, Massa Weldon, I ain't de bes' man fo' . . ."

"Don't interrupt me when I'm talking to you, boy! Now listen hard."

The master's voice droned on, but Samuel no longer heard him. Something strange was happening inside his mind. Things were coming back in a rush: Bible stories Jeremiah had told him of great men who did wonderful things. There was that fellow called Moses who parted the waves of the sea and led his people to freedom. Then a young buck named

David who wrestled with a lion and ended up as a king. And, yes, there was even a man named Samuel who, if the description held true, must have been some kind of a Praise House Watchman.

A thrill of excitement raced through Samuel's body like a bolt of lightning striking the top of a pine tree. Was it possible? Could he really be *that* kind of a man? He tried to calm himself. It wouldn't do to start stuttering and tripping over his own feet. "Ye'suh, massa, I is gwanna t'ink 'bout it."

Maum Beezie was alone on the piazza when Samuel stepped out into the cool evening air. She called to him quietly in the darkness. "Samuel," she said, "I ben sittin' in dis hey're rockin' chair thinkin' 'bout ma Jeremiah. Now I 'spect you gwanna t'ink I'm gettin' old an' a mite tetched in de h'ad, but listen ta what I gots ta say neber-de-less."

She leaned her head back and closed her eyes as she spoke. "It were like an angel be settin' hey're aside me, rockin' away in dat chair right ober dere." She pointed to the chair next to her.

Samuel glanced at the empty chair, half-expecting to see a white-robed angel sitting there.

"Now dis angel," continued the old woman, "he commences fer ta speak—in mah head, don' you know?" She opened her eyes and looked up at Samuel to make sure he was listening properly.

Samuel nodded, not knowing what else to do.

"Now dis-e-here angel, he tell me sumpin' 'bout you, onliest, I ain't too good at listnin' ta angel-talk, 'n I jes couldn't ketch it all. But what I did ketch went 'bout like-a dis . . ."

She hesitated again, then pushed herself up to look straight into Samuel's eyes.

"What he did say was: 'Samuel been chosen, jes like dat Samuel in de good Book. Dere be terr'ble times comin'—war an' famine an' pes'ilence.' You hear we talkin', chil'?"

"Yes'm, I hears you, Maum Beezie. I hears ebry word."

"Den keep on listnin', 'cause dat angel say mo'e. Say, 'De

Lawd lobe de Gullah folk jes as much as He lobe de white folk. Don' want no bad t'ing ta happen ta dose folk what He lobe.' "

"Yes'm, Maum Beezie, Gawd lobe de Gullah folk!" Samuel responded. He could feel the spirit moving in him now, just like when Jeremiah used to get all fired up with his preaching.

"Angel say, 'You tell dat Samuel—you tell him dis. Tell him he gots ta help take care ob de Lawd's people. Tell him dat he gots to keep 'em at peace 'cause de day ob deliberance is comin'!'"

Samuel was so stunned that he could hardly speak. "How— how I gwanna keep 'em at peace?"

The old woman fell back into her chair as though the effort of the last few minutes had sapped all her strength. The fire was gone from her, and her eyes closed as though in sleep. "It'll come ta you, boy," she said in a slow whisper. "By and by, it'll come ta you."

Samuel walked down the steps like one who had been struck dumb. How could *he* do these things? How could *he* keep the peace among his people if such terrible things were coming?

"Lawd," he prayed silently, "effen You really t'ink dat an ign'rant field han' an' a no-count slabe like me kin help make t'ings better, den I guess I be Yo man. Onliest I hope You understan' dat I ain't got much know-how 'bout such matters." He hesitated in his thoughts, hoping the Lord wouldn't think him presumptuous. "Kyan't speak near as good as Jeremiah done, but I's willing to learn. Fact ob de matter is, Lawd, guess You gwanna habe ta work me ober like a field what's neber been plowed."

A feeling of peace came over him. He was so deep in his own thoughts that, when Zach suddenly stepped from the shadows and fell in step with him, he jumped back in surprise.

The boy walked along quietly for several paces and then tugged at Samuel's shirt sleeve. "Be you gwanna do what de massa axe?"

"Mayhap, son. Jes mayhap I will."

"What he mean by all dem words 'bout de Gullah folk needin' you—an' de massa needin' you?"

Samuel stopped and looked down at Zach. Then he stretched out his arm and pointed to the dark horizon in the east. "See dat sky out der, boy?"

"Ye'suh, Mr. Samuel."

"Dat sky be 'bout black as my skin right now, hain't it?"

"Ye'suh."

"Afore de work bell ring in de mornin', you gets yo'self up an' go look at dat sky 'gin. First t'ing you gwanna see's de mornin' star jes twinklin' away as bright as kin be. You know what dat star mean?"

"Mean de mornin's comin'."

"Dat's right, boy. Dat star's a promise, sumpin' like de rainbow. It be a promise dat de dawn ob a new day gwanna break. Gullah folks hab a sayin' fer dat. You know what dat be?"

Zach nodded his head. "Ye'suh, Mr. Samuel. Dey calls it *day clean*."

"Um-hmm. Ain't dat de trut'!" Samuel knelt down and grasped Zach's arms firmly. Looking straight into the boy's eyes he added, "You an' me, son, an' all dem folks down in de quarters, we standin' right on de edge ob a clean, new day. Way I figger it, I's gwanna be up ta us ta use dat new day ta make t'ings a heap ob a lot bedder. You understan' what I's tellin' you, Zach?"

Zach could barely see Samuel's face in the darkness, but he felt the excitement in the man's grasp. "Yes, Mr. Samuel. I t'ink I knows what you is sayin'. Onliest t'ing is, how you gwanna keep de peace 'til de dawn come?"

Samuel stood up and let out a soft laugh. "Funny t'ing, but it jes come ta me. Gwanna start off by teachin' folks a new song. Matter ob fact, gwanna teach you dat song right now."

Samuel patiently went through the words, letting Zach repeat each stanza after him:

> Oh, stay in de field, chilluns,
> Stay in de field, chilluns,

Oh, stay in de field, chilluns,
'Til de war be ended.

I got my breastplate, sword, an' shield,
An' I'll go marchin' thro' de field,
'Til de war be ended.

Oh, my feet be shod wid de gospel grace,
An' 'pon my breast a shield;
An' wid my sword I inten' ta fight
'Til I wins de field.

"Dat's a mighty nice song, Mr. Samuel, but I likes de one 'bout de mornin' star a whole lot bedder. It gibs me a good feelin' right here." Zach tapped his chest for emphasis.

Samuel smiled and put his arm around Zach's shoulders. "Guess you be right, boy. It sho' nuff gibs me de same feelin'."

As man and boy walked down the dark trail packed hard by thousands of bare feet moving from cotton fields to slave quarters, the very trees echoed with the sound of their singing:

O de religion dat my Lawd gabe me,
Shine like a mornin' star.
O de religion dat my Lawd gabe me,
Shine like a mornin' star.
O brother you bedder
believe, believe.
O sister you bedder
believe, believe,
Ta shine like a mornin' star.

Bibliography

Allen, William F., Charles Ware, and Lucy Garrison, eds. *Slave Songs of the United States.* New York: Peter Smith, 1951.

Creel, Margaret. *A Peculiar People: Slave Religion and Community Culture Among the Gullah.* New York: University Press, 1988.

Dabbs, Edith M. *Sea Island Diary: A History of St. Helena Island.* Spartanburg, S.C.: The Reprint Co., 1983.

Daise, Ronald. *Reminiscences of Sea Island Heritage.* Orangeburg, S.C.: Sandlapper, 1986.

Genovese, Eugene D. *Roll, Jordan, Roll: The World the Slaves Made.* New York: Pantheon Books, 1974.

Georgia Writers' Project. *Drums and Shadows.* Athens: The University of Georgia Press, 1940.

Hurmence, Belinda, ed. *Before Freedom When I Just Can Remember: Oral Histories of Former South Carolina Slaves.* Winston-Salem: John Blair, 1989.

Jackson, Patricia Jones. *When Roots Die.* Athens: The University of Georgia Press, 1987.

Jones, Norrece, Jr. *Born a Child of Freedom, Yet a Slave: Mechanisms of Control and Strategies of Resistance in Antebellum South Carolina.* Hanover, N.H.: Wesleyan University Press, 1990.

Joyner, Charles. *Down by the Riverside: A South Carolina Slave Community.* Urbana: University of Illinois Press, 1984.

Lovell, John, Jr. *Black Song: The Forge and the Flame.* New York: Macmillan, 1972.

Plair, Sally. *Something to Shout About—Reflections on the Gullah Spiritual.* Mt. Pleasant: Molasses Lane, 1972.

Rosengarten, Theodore. *Tombee: Portrait of a Cotton Planter.* New York: Wm. Morrow & Co., Inc., 1986.

Smiley, Portia. "Folk-Lore From Virginia, South Carolina, Georgia, Alabama, and Florida." *Journal of American Folklore* 32 (July-September 1919): 357-383.